Worth Her Salt

*A Paranormal Women's Fiction Romance
Novel*

Stephanie Berchiolly

Author's Note

A big shout out to the many people who've supported me throughout my writing adventure:

Mandy Roth, Rick Migliore, Everly Rivers, Deb Carroll, Melissa DeGregorio, my amazing ARC Team, the reader group who are my lifeblood, and all the other wonderful individuals who've been so generous and inspirational along the journey of writing this book.

Words can't express how thankful I am to have you in my life!

Kelsey,
A bestie's friendship
is a magic that never
fades.

Editing by Linda Ingmanson

Cover Design by Mandy Roth

Description

Worth Her Salt

Sink or Swim. In high or low tide, will he be by your side?

————

We've landed in hot water again...

Florebelle's in trouble with only days to live.

My stress levels are through the roof. Between navigating my own relationship problems, protecting a defenseless little girl who needs my help, and harnessing magicks I don't understand, it's hard to travel light when packing such a heavy load.

I'm drowning in anxiety 24/7.

Will I be crushed by an overwhelming tsunami of vampires, ancient curses, and monumental family secrets?

Or will I get by with a lot of help from my friends...

and the guy trying his hardest to win me over?

Chapter One

Amira

I loved to look at the ocean. Look at, but not touch. Throughout my entire childhood, they had warned me away from the salty seas. My fear had gotten so bad, there were several years I wouldn't so much as take a bath, no matter how much Aunt Coral begged me to.

"It's just the salt water, hun. Don't go into the ocean. Fresh water's fine."

I'd never asked for more clarification on the matter. It was always just understood. Probably some silly fear passed down generation after generation. It didn't take a rocket scientist to figure out why some Black folk might not be super keen to jump into the ocean and go tooling around.

Don't get things twisted, I knew how to swim. I was, in fact, on the swim team in high school. Did well too, but there was always a healthy fear of sharks, undertows, and jellyfish holding me in check.

I pulled my knees up to my chest and sighed.

It might just be time to see a therapist to help work on these irrational fears. Heck, I live in Seattle after all, and that is smack dab right next to the ocean.

People here enjoyed the perfect summer weather by kayaking, gathering clams, and living their best lives in the three months where the sun shone and barely a drop of rain fell. It offset the other gray, rainy, and depressing nine months of the year.

But me?

I became paralyzed with fear whenever the word "ocean" popped up in casual conversation. Seemed like I spent more time avoiding it than I avoided scrubbing my toilet. And man, oh man, did I hate scrubbing my toilet.

A familiar pair of hands wrapped around my head, covering my eyes. I would have flinched if I didn't already have an inkling of who this flamboyant and touchy-feely person was.

"Guess who?" the voice asked as a tinkle of metallic jewelry made music behind me.

"Star, how did you find me?"

"No fair."

I turned to find Star pouting like a spoiled kid. "You always know it's me."

"Well, to be fair, no one else over the age of twelve has ever done that to me. So, it wasn't all that hard to figure out."

We laughed before removing our sandals, clasping hands, and making our way farther down the beach. Not too far, mind you, Star was quite aware of my fear of the water. The water itself might prove problematic to my fight-or-flight response, but I sure loved the feel of sand between my toes.

And, if I was being completely honest with myself, there was temptation. A titillating sense of danger tinged the alluring siren song that called out to me. That song was what frightened me the most.

Despite not wanting to go into the water, the closer I got to it, the more I wanted to dive in. There was also a nagging suspicion if I *were* to dive in, I wouldn't be coming back for quite some time—if ever.

"How did things go?" Star asked.

"Everything went smooth as butter. Her landlord let her out of the lease. I just used a bunch of legal mumbo jumbo. He didn't even put up a fight."

"Legal mumbo jumbo, you say? You sure you didn't hum a ditty and wrap him around your little finger?"

"Hah, maybe I did. But don't start with me, Star."

It was normal for us to fall back into comfortable conversation despite not seeing each other for several weeks. I got deeply entrenched in a backlog of divorce trials after our impromptu trip to visit Florebelle on her fortieth birthday.

Star flew off to the Goddess only knew where.

"Where were you off to while I was busting my butt at work? Gallivanting around the world with some prince or other on his royal yacht?" I pressed my finger to my lips in mock thought. "No, I'd bet my money on you hunting down exotic herbs to add to your latest batch of homemade hair care products."

Star rolled her eyes. Apparently, I'd hit a nerve. One of those guesses was most likely correct, but she probably wouldn't tell me now. She could be petulant that way. I was the type-A personality, and she was, well, a free spirit.

Back in the day, they would have said she gave off a hippy vibe.

Her long braids were gorgeous, with bits of golden jewelry woven in. She smelled like a field of wildflowers due to all the floral essences and oil extracts she used in her all-natural lotions and potions. It was a hobby she'd picked up back when we were kids. Probably the one positive remnant from the crazy cult she grew up in. They were all about self-sufficiency.

They weren't about anything anymore. Ten years after Star escaped their clutches for good, something forcibly disbanded them. That something was most likely a little government intervention.

I was eternally grateful the three of us had maintained our friendship over the decades, despite the insanity of our childhoods. We were all so similar and yet so different at the same time. Sisters of the heart—because we chose each other. In a way, that drew us ever closer together.

"Do you want to head to Alki Café, or should I invite myself over for dinner at your place?"

I could barely hear her words over the song of the ocean. This time, I swear the water was literally singing to me.

So beautiful.

"Do you hear that?" I asked.

She shook her head and picked up a sand dollar, scrubbing at the grit that clung to its nooks and crannies.

"Maybe we should go to your place, and I can cook something for you."

"You cook? No, thank you! I have a case tomorrow and can't afford to get food poisoning—again." I backed away, hands outstretched, waving frantically as I jokingly tried to ward her off. "No. Nay. Nope!"

This time, Star pouted in earnest. "The USDA says the internal temperature for pork should be one hundred forty-five degrees."

"Yes, but you didn't include the rest period, love. Carry-over cooking makes it as safe to eat as if it had reached one hundred sixty degrees. We're just lucky we didn't get trichinosis."

"What exactly is trichinosis?"

"It's a parasitic disease caused by worms—roundworms."

She blanched from repressed guilt. I had long ago forgiven her for the food poisoning. Had to take responsibility myself, to be honest. Letting Star cook meat, or anything that wasn't for body scrub or medicinal reasons, meant you were taking your life into your own hands.

Star grew up vegan and never quite figured out how to cook her animal brethren. Yeah, she thought she was related to everything.

I only let her cook for me that time because it was a special congratulatory meal to commemorate my graduation from law school.

Pretty sure that pork scare was the main reason I picked up my hobby in the culinary arts.

"Okay, sexy lady, let's head back to my place and I'll whip up some crepes. I have that brie you can't get enough of and a nice big bottle of bubbly a client left as a thank-you gift," I said.

"Mmm, that sounds lovely! We should go now. I'm pretty sure it's going to rain any minute."

We walked back to the car, with sandy feet, gales of laughter, and a hint of sadness because Florebelle wasn't chuckling right alongside us. Star and I hanging out with each other was nice, but not as nice as when we were all together.

The moment the car doors closed, the pitter-patter of raindrops descended upon the windshield.

"You're a freak. You know that, right?"

She knew I was kidding around, but damn. Star called it every single time. She was more accurate than the meteorologist on the KIRO 7 news.

"Freak in the sheets, you mean?" She gyrated seductively in the seat, shoulders bobbing, breasts bouncing, and golden hair trinkets flashing like sparks in the fading light.

5

"What am I going to do with you?" I started the car, head shaking from side to side as I tried to hold in my laughter.

———

"Please don't forget to wipe the sand off your feet before putting them on my brand-new couch." I gave Star the death glare to emphasize my point.

You know, the disapproving one mothers bestow upon their poorly behaved children. Along with a raised eyebrow and maternal feelings came a smidge of crankiness.

Last time we'd gone to the beach, I spent an hour vacuuming sand from between the couch cushions. Somehow, that sand became the gift that kept on giving. After several weeks of finding it in everything from shoes to a glass of water, my frustration mounted to the point I made the rash decision to buy brand-new furniture and hire a housecleaner.

One perk of being a spendthrift lawyer with no college debt: substantial discretionary funds and a propensity to buy a bunch of crap I didn't need. My only saving grace was rarely having enough free time to blow even *more* money on unnecessary purchases.

Gotta love that sweet, sweet retail therapy.

Hands freshly washed, ingredients poured into my Vitamix, I gave it a quick blitz before setting the crepe batter in the fridge to rest for an hour. I was reaching for the brie when I got a funny feeling I'd just gotten busted.

"Wow," Star proclaimed from the other room.

Crap, I should have locked the door. I would never hear the end of it now.

"Um, Amira, do we need to stage an intervention?"

Upon entering the craft room, I found Star with mouth

agape, eyes darting from side to side, taking in the thousands of balls of yarn I'd neatly divided by color, weight, and fiber.

There was even a computer dedicated to saving archived patterns, and a database that detailed every scrap of yarn I'd ever purchased. The walls were artfully lined with every color of the rainbow, and the custom-made bookshelves veritably groaned under the burdensome weight.

An enormous wooden loom was on display in the center of the room. She was my pride and joy. A Schacht standard floor loom with a weaving width of forty-five inches came with eight shafts. She was the first major purchase made after moving in.

Right now, she stood pristine and ready for my attention— freshly warped and ready to rock.

Admittedly, I wasn't a tremendous fan of the warping process. Warping a loom was a long and tedious job. On rare occasions, I'd go into a quasi-meditative state, but more often than not, it was an effort in futility that produced nothing but endless frustration.

Throughout my life, the only thing that carried me through the onerous undertaking was the joyous expectation of feeling yards upon yards of gorgeous yarn run through my eager fingers as I wove.

The whooshing sound of the wooden shuttle gliding through the warp threads and the soothing rhythm I created when adding the beater's syncopation.

Even the merest thought of weaving made me feel warm, giddy, and light. All the stresses of the day melted away and I thanked my lucky stars I happened across the class in college.

Who knew one weird elective would have such a positive long-term effect and ultimately become an object of obsession so many decades later?

Hell, if I weren't making decent money at my chosen profession, I couldn't feed my lavish yarn addiction.

Who knows what state I'd be in if I didn't have my guilty pleasure for relief.

Star sauntered over to the rigid heddle loom.

"Maybe one day you can show me how to use this one. It's small enough I should be able to handle it, and I'd sure love to get a taste of what you get from the craft."

"Of course. You know I'm happy to show you any time, but let's open up that bottle of champagne first."

"You know the way to my heart." She stopped halfway through the door, turning theatrically as she brought her right hand up into the air with a flourish. "Wine and cheese are ageless companions, like aspirin and aches, or June and moon, or good people and noble ventures."

"M. F. K. Fisher?"

"I have yet to stump you. How do you hold so many quotes in your head?"

"I don't know, girlie girl. It's a weird talent, I guess."

"Oh, speaking of our unique talents, I should do a reading for you tonight. It's been ages, and I feel in my bones something's coming round the bend. Something you need to be prepared for."

Shit on a shingle, I'd been having a similar feeling, but considered it to just be straight-up paranoia, maybe even an irrational fear borne from our somewhat deleterious adventures with Florebelle back in Maine.

After the utter insanity of other realms and very serious threats of death, we probably wouldn't be heading back to Orphic Cove any time soon.

Chapter Two

Florebelle

Arriving back in Orphic Cove after being gone for only a week proved almost as magickal as the first time she'd arrived. The wind was brisk, with a slight chill in the air. The smell of the sea left a salty tinge to each inhalation. It was all she could do to not run down the downtown sidewalk screaming, "I'm home!"

Her time away had gone better than expected, considering what she'd gone back to. A desolate apartment that positively reeked of the lies under which she'd lived for so many years. To make things worse, she later found out she'd been held captive by a series of spells woven to keep her docile and compliant.

Some magickal woo that stole away several good years of her life and made her think she was in a loving relationship with a frigging fairy.

Not just any fairy, but a fairy who was her nonrelated stepbrother, who absolutely despised her very existence. Stephen had called her a half-breed to her face, and happily

9

watched his mother, her stepmother, sentence her to death with not so much as a fare thee well.

Thinking about all those shenanigans at this point did nothing more than annoy her even further. She was having a pleasant moment, but the bitter memories born from her worst moments ground that pleasure away to nothing upon her initial arrival in Orphic Cove, just two months back.

After her breakup with Stephen, she had a week with some serious highs and insanity-inducing lows. The biggest high?

Jareth.

She couldn't wait to get back to the house and cuddle up next to him. Being gone for just one week to break the lease on her apartment in Maryland felt like she'd been away for an eternity. He'd wanted to go with her, but she felt a deep sense of shame at the mere idea of showing him what used to be her home.

Well, she'd thought of it as home, but everything that had happened there was a lie. Her safety zone had been nothing more than a prison. A prison of her own making, because she couldn't blame anyone else for her deciding to be with Stephen.

Star and Amira had both been extremely vocal in their disapproval, but no—she'd convinced herself she was *in love.*

She scoffed and ended up stomping down the sidewalk. The couple directly in her path jumped back, and she barreled through them without even registering their existence. The only noise was the wheels of her bag gliding down the sidewalk—their monotonous drone broken up by occasionally skipping over the dividing cracks.

Her reverie lasted until she made it to the Witch's House.

The black cat, a permanent fixture of the front porch, lay grooming himself on a white wooden chair. The muscles under his fur caused him to quiver in a good, long, luxurious stretch before he settled back into warming himself in a beam of sunlight streaming over his entire body.

This was the first time the darn thing hadn't hissed at her in a week. Perhaps today would be a good day. She'd just have to avoid any further thoughts of Stephen or near-death experiences.

Steppen.

She'd known him as Stephen.

Yet another lie.

Hand raised to the doorknob, it burst open just before she connected with the burnished metal. A familiar scent of warm fall spices and apple cider blew past her in a cozy, comforting breeze.

Before her stood old Mrs. Spigot. Short, compact, and fast as a jaguar on the hunt.

It never ceased to amaze her how a woman with such plump, tiny legs could travel so fast.

"Flora!" The dear, wee woman wrapped her in a colossal bear hug.

It had only been one week, but Mrs. Spigot greeted her as if she hadn't seen her for several years. Like a long-lost child returning to her family home just in time for the holidays.

Speaking of the holidays, Mrs. Spigot had really gone to town during her brief absence. There was a ten-foot, fully decorated Christmas tree right next to the reception desk. Underneath it lay piles upon piles of gaily wrapped presents.

How cute.

Mrs. Spigot also seemed to have gone more than a bit out of control with the red ribbon. Perhaps she had a penchant for tying bows and decided to let her freak flag fly, because there were around five hundred of the things scattered about.

Somehow, she made it look quite tasteful.

Glittering silver, gold, green, red, and metallic blue bulbs sparkled in the sunlight streaming through the large front windows. The vision made her smile. The festivity of it all reminded her how much she'd been looking forward to spending Christmas here in Orphic Cove with Mrs. Spigot and Jareth.

Where is Jareth?

"He'll be back soon, dear. Had to pop over to the other side for a quick visit."

Darn, she'd really been looking forward to being swept up by him. The memory of how they met for the first time caused her face to grow hot.

She'd burst out of the train's bathroom in a mad panic, tripped, and had literally fallen into his powerful arms.

Well, that might not be one-hundred-percent accurate, but it was close enough. They started out as complete strangers and ended up saving each other—in more ways than one.

Their chance encounter led to a lifetime of possibilities.

Though, some of them, like Steppen, otherwise known as Stephen, and his crazy mother, hell-bent on ending Florebelle's life, weren't the most positive things to dwell on.

Dammit, no more fairy shizz. Stick to the now.

Mrs. Spigot was nowhere in sight. Florebelle really had to stop wandering around in the hallways of her mind. The poor woman was likely to think she was ungrateful, not happy to see her, or just plain rude. Though she highly suspected she'd considered none of those things.

Florebelle Fairfield picked up her bag and headed upstairs to her room. There was no need to check in here. To most, it was a B and B, but to her, it was home. She wasn't quite clear on the details of how that worked out, but Mrs. Spigot had never charged her so much as a red cent and had explicitly told her in no uncertain terms that she lived there now.

To be honest, she wasn't altogether sure there hadn't been another damned glamour, or a hex placed on her. Either way, she was fine with it, because the food here was wonderful, and the company she kept made her realize what she'd been missing all her life.

Midnight, and she still couldn't sleep. She could only assume Jareth had gone back home to the fairy realm. Time moved differently there. She hadn't quite been able to figure out exactly how differently it worked. There didn't seem to be much rhyme or reason to it.

Once, they'd visited his childhood home for what felt like half a day—fae realm time—but when they arrived back in Orphic Cove, three whole days had passed.

On another occasion, they stayed in the fairy realm for a week. When they came back from that visit, she found they'd only been away three days.

The last two times she tried to figure out the mechanics of the time difference, she got a migraine. After that, she just stopped trying to make sense of it altogether.

Florebelle grabbed a candle from the table in the hallway. There was no point turning on the light, as there was enough coming from the moon to see large objects.

She felt compelled to go to the fifth floor of the massive house.

Her slippers made dull thunking sounds on the bare wooden stairs of the silent house as she made her way up, up, up.

It wasn't long before she found herself standing in front of a rather innocent-looking door—much like the kind in her cheap apartment back in Maryland. She couldn't help but chuckle. Everything in this house was old and unique.

It tickled her to no end thinking about someone replacing antique doors with an inexpensive, economic, hollow core from the local Home Depot.

The day before leaving to break her lease in Maryland, she'd felt a strong desire to enter this room. She hadn't thought about the urge since, but here she was, standing here.

Had something kept me away from it until tonight?

Curiosity piqued, she stood in the hallway, about to enter a mysterious door on the fifth floor of the Witch's House?

What could possibly go wrong?

Chapter Three

Amira

"Do you always carry tarot cards with you, just in case?" I asked, while settling into the comfy leather chair across from Star.

"Yep, never leave home without 'em." She made finger guns and clicked her tongue in time as she pretended to shoot. I rolled my eyes at her silliness.

Star shuffled the deck.

The soft fluttering of the cards as they intermixed in rapid succession was a sound I found soothing. Having heard it a million times throughout the course of our relationship, it was an automatic signal for me to go into relaxation mode.

I scooped up the universal remote from the coffee table and pressed a few buttons.

The lights dimmed, the fireplace roared to life, and the soft tones of meditative music played in the background at a volume so low, it was barely audible.

Star had taught me sound, smells, and all the senses, really, could play into a reading.

She'd been right about way too many things over the years. Things I never truly understood. I long ago realized it was easier to listen to her on this front, at least.

We all had our lanes, and tarot was definitely not one of mine.

It was a two-way street, as I wouldn't take too kindly to Star meddling in my weaving or cooking affairs. The practices of cartomancy and anything to do with spirits were topics I instantly deferred to her on.

"All right, baby cakes, you know the drill." Star handed the deck of cards over to me.

It took longer than usual to form the right question in my mind.

I typically went for specific, pointed questions, but much like Star, I felt something monumental was brewing and I needed a big-picture view.

With the deck in hand, I repeated my question over and over again while shuffling, tapping, and imbuing whatever bits of me I could to get as accurate a reading as possible.

I divided the cards into uneven piles, placing a stack on the coffee table, facedown, leaving three piles.

"You locked on to what you want me to read for?"

"Yes," I said solemnly and gave a curt nod, while still repeating the question in my mind. It was a habit I'd formed over the years. Repeat the question like a mantra until the last card is drawn.

Star wouldn't speak to me again until the spread was complete and everything was laid out on the coffee table.

What does my future hold?

I closed my eyes and concentrated on the question. Holding it in my mind was the most important thing. Gone were the worries about my upcoming case, or Star discovering my stash of yarn, which had grown to epic hoarder levels.

Even the settling crepe batter in the fridge was a distant memory.

The sound of the deck being reassembled into a single pile was cut by the gentle swish of individual cards being removed from the deck. I heard Star's fingernails lightly tap on the wood as she laid them down one by one.

The ritual was perfectly timed to the relaxing music playing in the background—chimes and bells as light and airy as butterfly wings.

What does my future hold?

She drew two cards. I didn't count them as much as I had a gut feeling about the number she pulled.

When she laid the second card on the table, she gasped.

My eyes flew open.

It was unusual for Star to react so dramatically during a tarot card reading, or at anything else, to be perfectly honest. She was always a pretty "go with the flow" type of person who wasn't often rattled. About the only times she turned into a drama queen, there were hormones, hot water bottles, and cramps involved.

"Is something wrong?"

"I wouldn't say wrong, but"—she pulled her eyes away from the cards and reluctantly locked on to mine—"both cards are Major Arcana."

"Should I be worried?"

"No, no, of course not. It's just a reading. Plus, I'm not done yet. Go back to thinking about your question." I closed my eyes and drifted back into a quasi-meditative state.

What does my future hold?

I heard the friction of the last card sliding against the wood of the table as she put it down into the last position of the three-card spread.

The cards laid before me were all I could see when I

opened my eyes and took them in. I didn't even seem to have peripheral vision anymore.

"The first card is your current situation. It's the Tower."

"Uh-oh." I tensed at the prospect. Though I didn't have the cards memorized completely, I knew this one was best reversed. It stood up loud and proud, defying me to resist its depiction of a tower plunged in flames. Oh, and not to forget the people jumping out of windows to their deaths. "Yeah, that card looks super hopeful."

"It just means you're going to have some upheaval in your life. The Death card's usually collective and impersonal. So, it doesn't exactly mean you're about to have a personal tragedy or anything. I'd think of it more like..." She paused as if to choose her words carefully, "transformation. You're an agent of transformation. Change is coming, but it's probably not all bad."

"You know I hate change. Especially if I can't control it."

Star sat back and laughed so hard, she snorted. Of course, her snort made me crack up as well. It took her quite some time to catch enough breath to squeak out a sentence. "You and change aren't exactly besties!"

"Yes, yes. Okay. Now back to the reading. 'Cause the towering inferno paired with a devil isn't exactly giving me a mad case of the warm fuzzies." My voice trailed off as I raised an eyebrow, wondering how Star was going to spin this.

"Well, this second card is your current obstacle, and yes, it's the Devil. He mostly signifies the taboo. Your shadow side's going to come out and play." She glanced up with concern, causing the skin around her eyes to wrinkle for a split second. She wiped the emotions away so fast, I wondered if I'd imagined what I saw. "You need to be honest with yourself. Express your true emotions, even in anger."

"Yeah, that totally goes well in a court of law. Should I

throw something at the judge the next time they rule against my client? Perhaps a slew of expletives flung at one of the partners at the firm the next time they give me a last-minute priority case that has me staying in the office until five a.m. to catch up on five million metric tons of paperwork?"

I was only half joking. Anger was an emotion I usually kept bottled up.

Honestly, about the only feeling I let out on the regular was steely determination—if that was even an emotion.

It was rare to let happiness seep out the raw, tender edges when I wasn't with my girls. Emotions had no place in the world of justice.

And I had been born and bred for my profession.

"Anyway," Star said gruffly. I could tell I was annoying her with my constant onslaught of negativity, but could you blame a girl after getting a towering inferno and a frigging demon? She cleared her throat passive-aggressively before continuing, "The third card is your future."

"Okay, this one looks more promising." I grimaced. "Except she's upside down."

"The Empress represents the natural world. Reversed typically symbolizes the more violent of emotions triggered by ignorance or people acting hella stupid. Don't go too far with your emotions and your need for justice, or you might destroy the things you enjoy."

"Such is my daily life, but I'm confused because the previous card"—I couldn't bring myself to say The Devil—"gave me strict instructions to follow my anger. This one is telling me that following said anger would likely harsh my mellow?"

"Yeah. She's pretty much just warning you not to go too far. Otherwise known as: Don't be a d-bag, Amira."

With the tension broken by her joke, we both laughed.

I could be the queen of d-bags when I was in court, but that version of me was calm, cool, and collected. If necessary, I could rip a person to shreds without a hint of remorse.

Using my powers for evil had much more detrimental effects in my life.

"Okay, so you're talking about that time I made that boy piss his pants, right?"

Star stopped laughing as suddenly as she started. The hand that came out to sweep up the cards faltered from a nervous tremor.

Odd.

Before I had a chance to ask what was going on, she dropped the cards into their velvet bag and sauntered toward the hallway.

"Gotta pee. Be right back."

What perfect timing. As soon as Star rounded the corner, I realized I was more affected by the reading than I'd thought.

My snarky comments had masked the nagging sense of dread I'd been feeling over the past few days.

"Son of a bitch," I muttered into the now-empty room.

Still reeling from the read, I felt like I'd been punched in the stomach and held underwater. It was hard to catch a good, deep breath.

Am I wheezing? Yes. Where's my inhaler?

I fumbled around, looking for my rescue inhaler. All I could find was the maintenance one.

Crap.

This was no doubt psychosomatic. I took a hit of Alvesco and held my breath for the required ten or so seconds. It wouldn't do much for me now, but I was hoping, much like a Pavlovian response, my lungs might relax once I went through the ritual of systematically inhaling and holding my breath.

Fortunately, it worked.

Star seemed completely oblivious to my panic-induced asthma attack when she returned.

Instead of drawing this moment out any longer with follow-up questions, I decided it would be best to drop it and focus on dinner.

That would give us both plenty of time to get some distance and not approach the reading from an emotional place. I didn't handle emotions particularly well, and she didn't handle my not handling emotions particularly well.

Unfortunately for me, as I went into the kitchen to assemble our meal, I was hit with an onslaught of memories.

Memories I preferred to keep hidden.

———

My first memory was of a strange house. I don't think I'd been there for very long, and I was fairly certain I was insanely young when I lived there.

So young, in fact, I wasn't altogether sure it wasn't a false memory.

The strange house had very few details to go with it. All I remembered was the smell of dust and an almost endless sea of wood. All the furniture was wood; the walls were covered in wood paneling. I also had the distinct impression the room or the very building itself was massive.

I'm pretty sure I'd taken my first steps here, surrounded by other kids ranging from infants to teenagers.

Then my mind was full of memories of my aunties. Serafina, Josefina, Delfina, and Coral. The first three were identical triplets.

Coral was their sister, but would answer no questions about whether she was older or younger. She kept her past pretty well hidden, but I was sure she'd been adopted—much like me.

We were all obviously related in some way, but Aunt Coral, who I called Aquafina, and I were sort of the black sheep of the family.

Though I didn't know her age, Coral appeared to be considerably younger than her sisters. Closer to my age.

Another trait we shared was our darker skin. We both had one foot in the realm of the Aunties and another firmly planted in Black culture.

We also had the same nose.

She was the one who most often drilled into my head that I was to stay away from the ocean. I could only swim in fresh water because of my delicate constitution—an issue she was also afflicted with.

That's probably where I came up with the nickname Aquafina for her. She wasn't impressed.

In fact, she absolutely loathed it.

Being compared to a brand of drinking water was bad enough, though things got better when the rapper Awkwafina came on the scene. She loved to sing "My Vag" at every opportunity for about four years.

Despite having a beautiful singing voice, or because of it, her belted rendition of the song made Thanksgivings and Christmases insanely awkward.

"Do you think we've ever been to Orphic Cove before?" I absently asked Star. I was almost as startled by the question as she was. The words popped out before I'd even fully formed them in my mind.

I wasn't the kind of person to speak without thinking first.

She sat up bolt upright and looked away. Star looked positively cagey, definitely not a good sign.

This was one of her tells when she was trying to hide something.

"That B and B seemed awfully familiar. Reminded me of the large room I told you about remembering from when I was a kid. Yeah, I know it's strange and highly unlikely, but there's something about it that just seems so damned familiar. And I can't put my finger on *why.*" I waited for a reply. She continued to act like she hadn't heard me. "Star?"

"Hm?"

"Did the B and B in Orphic Cove seem familiar to you? I mean, you still sometimes get lost in my apartment, which you've visited at least a hundred times, but you seemed to know your way around town when we were there."

"Well, uh." She dug around in her bag before producing a triumphant grin. "I almost forgot to give you this. Surprise!" She pulled out a single ball of yarn. It was a fuzzy bluish-gray color, and I instantly yearned to caress it.

"Ohhh," I squealed. "Yarn? Where did you get it?"

"A small seaside town in the UK. I forgot to bring it the last time I came over. They only had the one ball, or skein, or whatever it is you call these things, but I just *knew* you'd go absolutely cuckoo bananas over it."

I reached out to snatch up my prize.

It reminded me of the ocean on a gray fall day. The wool was soft and light. It would make a wonderfully warm scarf or shawl if I could find another skein from the same lot.

Otherwise, I had a couple of others in the same weight I could pair it with. They would accent it nicely!

My mind raced with possibilities as I gleefully grinned.

"Thank you, Star. You're the best."

It wasn't until she was heading out the door two hours later, full of crepes, cheese, and champagne, that I realized she'd distracted me—like a cat with a ball of yarn—and sneaked off without answering my earlier question.

Very suspicious indeed.

Chapter Four

Florebelle

The room was pitch-black. An inky darkness so thick, a candle wouldn't make a dent. It absorbed all life and light like a vacuum. That wasn't even the worst part. The eerie quiet made her stop where she stood, half in, half out of the room. Afraid to take that last step and commit to fully entering the ominous space.

She took a deep breath and strode forward with false confidence.

BAM!

The door slammed shut of its own accord.

Held still by fear, Florebelle stood poised on her toes like a deer, eyes gradually growing accustomed to the darkness. All she could make out were the largest objects on the periphery of the room—dresser to the right, a bed to the left. She was almost certain a massive armoire was directly in front of her against the opposite wall.

She shuffled to the window, drawing back the curtain. The moon's feeble light was just enough to make the room seem somewhat less frightening. Now that there was light, she was left with the realization the ambient sounds were so muted, it was a near-perfect silence.

No. Wait.

There was a rather faint keening coming from somewhere nearby, but Florebelle couldn't quite make out the direction.

Maybe it was just a ringing in her ears.

It grew incrementally louder until it crescendoed to an ear-piercingly high-pitched whine. She slammed her hands over her ears to block the sound.

Eventually, it ceased.

She shrugged it off and retraced her steps, fumbling as she felt her way along the wall beside the door, hoping to find a light switch.

Probably should have done that first, dumb-dumb brain.

Someone, or something, clamped onto her shoulders with a viselike grip.

"Let me go!" Florebelle screamed into the night.

They'd bound her. Tied her up and left her to rot alone in the darkness. The stink of ozone and spent electricity clung thick in the air, burning her nose. The rough, unforgiving cobblestone floor beneath her buckled and writhed.

She visualized it as opening lips, a portal to a toothy maw, ready to swallow her up like so much fresh meat.

Her skin both burned and tingled, as if she were being simultaneously kissed by the flames of a raging fire and doused with ice water.

"No! Oh please, God, no!"

She was falling, falling.

The empty air whooshed around her as she slid down the

gullet of an invisible monster, struggling against the bindings that lashed her wrists together. The fight didn't last long before she collapsed in a shivering heap, where she felt the soft press of warm flesh beneath her fists.

Both hands lashed out. She grabbed at that warmth with panicked determination, literally holding on for dear life.

"Florebelle, wake up!"

A familiar voice beckoned her from far away. She shook even more violently, wrapped up in a thick cloak of animalistic fear, the rush of adrenaline slowly dying down as she realized she was no longer fighting for her life.

Something warm pressed against her side and gently rocked her awake. Tangled up in a sheet, goose bumps over every square inch of her skin, Florebelle had broken out in a cold sweat.

She was confused. Scared.

"What... What happened?"

"You had a nightmare." Jareth wrapped her in his powerful arms. Whatever terrors she'd been wrestling with drifted away.

"It was just a dream?" she asked. Her voice came out in a childlike whisper of relief and disbelief.

With recent nightmares fast fading away, she fell back asleep in Jareth's sturdy arms. This time, when she slipped back into the world of dreams, things were considerably more peaceful.

The frame of her dreamscape was filled by Jareth's kind eyes, his full lips broken out in a warm, loving smile as he moved toward her in slow motion and covered her with kisses.

"That was the third time this week, and it's only Tuesday." Jareth raised a concerned eyebrow. He stared at her while buttering his toast.

"I've never been prone to nightmares."

"These are more than mere nightmares. If I didn't heal as quickly as I do, I'm sure the local authorities would start asking questions about who was beating the crap out of me every night." He gave her a playful wink. As if jokes about domestic abuse charges against Black women were funny.

"Well, perhaps we should sleep in separate beds for a while. I don't want to end up living the dream of three hots and a cot." Her voice lowered menacingly. The knowledge that she was being overly hostile and defensive didn't elude her. She just didn't care. "Maybe we should try different rooms until I can figure this out."

He dropped his toast onto the plate and leaned back in his seat. Florebelle could tell he wasn't exactly thrilled with the outcome of the conversation. Part of her wanted to drop it and take back what she'd said. Which made her question whether her wanting to drop it and move on was an act of free will, or just another fairy spell used to manipulate her into compliance.

She put her head in her hands, elbows resting on the table.

Not today, Satan. I will not let the demons of the past ruin a good thing.

The screech of Jareth's chair as he pushed back from the table startled her. There wasn't even the hint of footsteps between the sound of the chair and the moment he placed a hand on her shoulder and squeezed reassuringly.

At times like these, Jareth was often at a loss for what to say or do, but he never just ran away or remained silent. He always made sure she knew he was there for her, no matter how grumpy and unpleasant she might be.

Something was wrong. Night terrors and irrational suspicions had never been her thing.

She'd been pulling back lately. Pulling back a lot.

This was a new relationship, and things would be tentative for a while. That was normal. But she couldn't let the tarnish of the recently failed romance with her ex ruin a great thing in its infancy. Jareth was a good man.

Correction: Jareth was a good fairy.

Perhaps it's time to see a therapist?

She wondered what she'd even say.

"Hi, my name's Florebelle Fairfield, and I'm half fairy. I'm the rightful heir to the Seelie Court, in fact. Oh, I almost forgot —the current fae queen and my ex-boyfriend/stepbrother who isn't actually remotely related to me are probably plotting my death right now."

Yep, that sounded one-hundred-percent legit. A seasoned mental health professional definitely wouldn't try to have her institutionalized or, at the very least, heavily medicated and monitored for a very, very long time.

Her greatest fear was ending up like Star.

Right before college, one of her best friends had ended up in a place like that. Her foster parents took her in because she was seeing and hearing things. Once she got out, she never talked about it again.

If anyone tried to bring it up, she'd clamp down so tight, it was like pulling teeth to even get her to acknowledge your existence. Florebelle and Amira had stopped asking years ago because they knew it must have been bad—as in trauma-inducing bad—because Star had never met a secret she didn't have a problem divulging, in vivid detail. No matter how little the person on the receiving end wanted to know it.

Star had no shame. And damn, did Florebelle ever admire her for that.

Jareth placed both hands on her cheeks and was gazing at her with *The Look*. That look of love and adoration that completely made her melt inside. This time, things were different.

When she focused and saw the intensity, she didn't melt at all.

She froze up.

Body rigid, Florebelle sighed and removed one of his hands from her face. She lightly clasped it in her right hand like it was a dead fish, before forcing herself to place her left hand atop it.

Poor Steppen, why he puts up with me, I'll never know.

Steppen?

Holy shit, did I just call my current boo by my duplicitous, manipulative ex's name?

She panicked.

Hand dropped, Florebelle jumped up from the chair so quickly, it crashed to the ground. With the clatter of the chair ringing fresh in her ears, she noticed Jareth's shock. Her cheeks burned with shame.

Florebelle's eyes welled with tears as her heart beat faster and faster.

If she stayed any longer, she was going to pass out or throw up. She had to get out of there—fast!

She ran from the room as swiftly as her legs could carry her. Full of confusion, denial, embarrassment, and disgust, Florebelle was nearly blinded by the upwelling of powerful emotions. She was so hell-bent on getting away from Jareth, she almost plowed right into Mrs. Spigot on her way past the front desk as she raced to the hallway toward the stairwell.

Mrs. Spigot's cherubic smile fell. The woman was a saint.

Could witches be saints?

Well, if they could, then Mrs. Spigot was one of them. Either that or with her advanced age came the ability to mask her true feelings at all times.

Her hair fell in a soft layered bob that framed her well-worn, round face. Almost any time Florebelle saw her, she felt instantaneously happy, but not today.

Today, there was no reciprocal smile, just the stink of pure panic and the sting of tears that were about to lose their hold on her lower eyelids.

"Are you okay, dear?" the gray-haired woman asked with concern as she laid a full armload of freshly laundered sheets on the reception desk.

"Yeah, I'm good." It felt weird lying to her, so she quickly retracted the statement. "No, I don't think I am. Just wish there were therapists for fae folk. I feel like I'm going bonkers, but if I talk to someone outside this house about what's happened over the past few weeks, they'd likely lock me up and throw away the key."

Mrs. Spigot squinted slightly as she sank into deep thought.

"Well, there's always Mrs. Pettigrew. She knows about witches, and fae and..." She paused suspiciously. "Well, she knows about everything and won't lock you up anywhere. Unless you're breaking one of the Five Laws."

"The Five Laws?" As soon as the question left Florebelle's mouth, she realized she had no desire to know what any of those laws were, even if it was in her best interest to do so. She also realized they were very close to the dining room and Jareth had exceptional hearing. "Ummm, Mrs. Spigot, I was thinking about going back to my old room for a while. Would that be okay?"

"Of course, dear. This house is yours." She chuckled and

31

shook her head as she swooped up the pile of clean, white cloth from the desk. The scent of fresh laundry dried in the sun wafted up briefly before Florebelle blinked, and she was gone.

She had no idea how that woman moved faster than an Olympic runner, but who was she to question it after all the strange things she'd come across since moving to Orphic Cove —finding out fairies and witches existed, and falling in love with a fae dude ten seconds after breaking up with another fae dude.

Prince of the fae, at that!

It was as if her fortieth birthday—which had happened just three short weeks ago—had been the gateway to an entire universe of crazy she was completely unequipped to handle.

Fortunately, she didn't have to deal with all that crazy alone. She had Jareth. But their relationship was too new and too fresh to lay all her issues on him at this early stage.

That was what her girls were for. A bond of friendship forged through decades of shared secrets and inner thoughts they wouldn't tell anyone outside their tight little crew.

Amira and Star, her best friends in the entire world, had surprised her by flying out to Orphic Cove on her fortieth birthday. What was supposed to be a postbreakup, birthday-weekend-getaway, celebration fest turned into a life-or-death adventure she'd survived only because of them. After the shit hit the fan and things calmed down a bit, her friends had flown back to Seattle.

They'd gone home, and she'd stayed in the weird little town in Maine she'd only heard about because her ex-fiancé was going to bring her here—no doubt to murder her.

Florebelle shook her head, and her whole body followed. The temporary release of tension brought her stress levels down one, maybe two notches.

She made her way to the stairwell to pack up in preparation for moving back to her old room.

That wouldn't be all she needed to unpack. She and Jareth still had a lot to talk about regarding personal truths never divulged throughout the month or so they'd been together.

Like how her besties were straight-up witches. Yes, they'd always been interested in the woo, but she'd never known they had actual powers.

Hell, she never knew she had powers until she and her besties were upstairs doing travel spells to save Jareth from the clutches of the batshit-crazy Seelie queen.

Their next few girls' nights were going to be heaps of fun while they talked about arcane stuff she'd have thought was fiction prior to her recent education, trial-by-fire style. She'd also have to get to the bottom of how Star and Amira knew she was a witch, yet had never bothered to tell her.

That wasn't completely true. They'd tried to involve her in their spells and incantations in the past, but Florebelle had pointedly told them, on several occasions, that she wasn't remotely interested in their shenanigans.

Okay. Make that every single occasion... Ever.

It was hard not to be upset and feel betrayed, but it was also difficult to blame them. They'd waited for her to catch up, had given her more than enough time to figure it out for herself, and never tried to pressure her into admitting or claiming something she wasn't ready for.

Still, they'd have to talk about it.

Right before opening the doorway to the stairwell, Florebelle held her hands out and wiggled her fingers.

There's magicks inside me. I wonder what else I don't know?

In the meantime, it might be best for her to focus on more

33

current, pressing concerns. It was time to stop pussyfooting around.

She needed to go to the room she shared with Jareth.

No. I need to go to Jareth's room. It's time to move out.

Her involuntary sigh positively oozed melancholy, but she steeled herself for the task.

After I'm done, I can get settled into my old room and get tidied up before calling that Mrs. Pettigrew lady Mrs. Spigot recommended.

It was time to set up that appointment.

She took a deep, not-so-steady breath and twisted the knob, resigned and ready to make a new start.

Chapter Five

Amira

Something at the back of my mind was nagging at me when I woke up the next day. It lingered there long after I departed for work. Normally, insignificant things like this would drift away when another tort case or pile of legal paperwork landed on my desk.

Unfortunately for me, I knew from the moment I woke up that today wasn't fated to be a normal day.

I made no fewer than a hundred mistakes before lunch, the biggest of which was nearly forgetting an important meeting with a lower-level office functionary. It turned out the person I almost inadvertently blew off was from HR.

It was likely some issue or another with an intern.

I'd been brought in for questioning once before after some idiot who couldn't hold his liquor "accidentally" patted a legal secretary's bottom at the Christmas party.

Arriving in the assigned conference room out of breath and flustered, I was only half paying attention when the straight-backed long-haired blonde woman asked me a pretty serious question right out of the gate.

"Have you ever witnessed sexual harassment here at Bankton, Rockman, Hughes, and Wins?"

"Sexual harassment?" I asked.

This was a pretty loaded question I wasn't prepared for and really didn't want to get into right now, but then again, who wanted to have a discussion with an HR rep about sexual harassment in the workplace?

It didn't take a rocket scientist to figure out who the prime suspect was—good old George Wins. His ironic last name must at least have been partially responsible for his cheesy-assed attitude. The man couldn't take any situation seriously, and he gave compliments to women in a way that was never particularly flattering.

There had been a time or two I'd been at the receiving end, and all I can say was that I wanted a skin-scorching hot shower to wash away the taint of his words.

How he'd become a partner was anyone's guess. Every employee of the female persuasion was surprised he hadn't been fired or disbarred long ago because George was a giant walking liability.

Most of us wondered if he had blackmail material on the other partners—Scott Bankton, Shawn Rockman, or Eli Hughes.

Having the big three shielding him was the only reason we could come up with to explain why the man was still gain-fully employed here.

That being said, I was almost certain this was about something else.

Most times, I was alone in a room with him, I glimpsed his aura. It was as black as the dark side of the moon. His aura wasn't just black.

It was dark, dingy, and dangerous.

If someone were to tell me George had no soul, I wouldn't be surprised. The man always gave me a major case of the chills.

Last time he was behind me in a staff meeting, my skin didn't stop crawling for over half an hour. It was as if I could feel that oily aura of his creeping up on me whenever my back was turned.

He reminded me of the Weeping Angels in *Doctor Who*.

Every time I turned around, he got closer. But you could never hear his footsteps.

I was afraid to blink when he was around, scared that in that fraction of a second, I'd feel his breath on the back of my neck, and that would be the last thing I ever felt.

Ever since I was a child, I'd been pretty good at playing things off—I was a lawyer, after all—but that man was as evil as evil gets, and quite frankly, he scared the shit out of me.

For the most part, George had never done anything bad to me. There'd been no reason for me to file anything formal against him. And to my knowledge, no one else had dared to lodge any major complaints.

So color me surprised to not just hear about a sexual harassment claim coming up, but also being called into an office to talk about it.

Of course, it might have been someone, or something, else.

Hell, it might have been me.

I *did* give our intern, Maribeth Cummings, a gag gift when she told us she was engaged. She'd gotten more than a little tipsy a few weeks back after a work outing and mentioned something about her fiancé's "endowment." So, I got her a coffee mug that said "Well endowed."

The problem came from Maribeth not remembering she'd told us this little gem about her man, coupled with her unfortunate last name and the fact she'd been blessed with ginormous breasts.

Maybe I didn't think that one through.

Sue me.

Oops!

"Yes, sexual harassment, but don't worry. These interviews are completely anonymous. Nothing you say here will get back to any of your fellow employees."

Despite her reassurances, I was pretty certain it would get back to Bankton, Rockman, and/or Hughes at some point. Most of us acted like the rooms in the office were bugged, because they seemed privy to all kinds of conversations that happened without them in the room.

It was easier to think the rooms were bugged than to consider there was a narc among us.

"Well, this is the sort of thing I'd need some time to think about. I've been here for over twelve years and you kind of sprang this on me. Ms.... I'm sorry. I don't know if I ever caught your name."

"I completely understand. My name is Angela Dimwitty." Her face was bland and blank, with no hint of a smile or even a smidgen of personality. Something about this situation didn't seem right, but Dimwitty?

It took every ounce of composure honed after decades of practicing my best deadpan, stony-faced stare in courtrooms not to burst into laughter. I couldn't even begin to imagine what torment she suffered through in high school.

Nope. Stop it. Don't think about it. Just say what you have to say to get the hell out of here.

"I'll reach out to you if anything comes to mind."

She gave one brisk nod as she stood. Once out of the chair, she froze in place, not moving a muscle. Her cold, blank eyes lay on me like a dead fish.

It didn't take long to translate the universal signal of "Get Out."

She had no further use for me. Thank goodness.

Dimwitty.

Fortunately, her name didn't pop back into my mind until I was well past the conference room doors. With a hand abruptly placed to my lips, I hid the involuntary titter that escaped with a lame, fake cough.

———

Settled at my desk, I went back to my briefs. I had too much to do before heading to court this afternoon.

Boy, was it going to be a doozy.

My ability to compartmentalize had always been an immense advantage in my field, and life in general. It was a necessity in my line of work, but in this case? There was something about it that made it not just bust through my defenses. It shattered them to bits like a grenade.

Rat-a-tat-tat.

Only one person I knew knocked like that.

Carter.

The first thing I saw when I looked up was his shaved head and inquisitive eyes peering through the glass above my nameplate on the door.

He was one big, tall, glass of dark chocolate milk—the decadent kind you order in a fancy restaurant.

Pretty sure he drank plenty of the stuff when he was a kid, 'cause he grew up big and strong.

His suit was so tight in the arm and thigh areas, I swore one good flex and he would rip the fabric to shreds, like Bruce Banner becoming the Hulk.

Another thing I admired was that Carter never missed leg day. You could crack a walnut between those cheeks.

Maybe I'd get lucky and catch another surreptitious glimpse of his perfectly formed tooshie. His suit jacket often covered it up, but there had been multiple occasions I was blessed enough to catch more than a quick glimpse.

Ok, perv, try to act normal.

I waved him in. As soon as the door opened, he bounded toward me like an excited deer.

"Today's the big day, huh?"

"Yep, I'm just finishing up some last-minute work before heading to court."

"Well, I don't mean to interrupt. Had a few minutes and thought I'd pop over to see if you needed any help." His eyes twinkled above his perfect big white smile.

"I'm good. Do appreciate the offer, though. You were a great paralegal back before you went to law school."

We laughed as I took a jog down memory lane, thinking about the time we first met.

The contents of a box full of papers I carried had gone flying when I tripped over my giant clown feet.

Carter had swooped in for the assist.

Not only did he help pick up the scattered debris and put everything back into its cardboard home, but he went with me to my tiny cubicle and helped me reorganize it all.

We were together for nearly two hours, and that was two hours after he was supposed to have headed home for the night.

He'd always been there for me through thick and thin. If circumstances had been different, we might have made a good team outside the office as well as inside it.

With just a handful of years of legal experience more than

me, instead of trying to get in as a partner at the firm, he fought for *me* to earn that title.

Whereas everyone else was in competition for the prestigious position, it didn't take long to realize it wasn't one of Carter's life goals.

He wasn't built like the rest of us, and boy, did I ever find that refreshing.

I reached for a pen as a distraction from my thoughts about Carter.

Big mistake.

When the pen hit the floor, I accidentally kicked it several feet away in my haste in trying to retrieve it.

Damnable giant clown feet!

Maybe it wasn't such a big mistake after all, because Carter, ever the gentleman, bent over to pick it up for me.

Mmmm.... That ass!

The view made me wonder what other places I could bounce pennies off on his taut, muscular body.

I almost cheered out loud when the fabric of his pants strained so hard, I thought it would definitely rip! But, just in the nick of time, he pulled himself upright, pen in hand.

"You always seem to drop things around me. I'm starting to wonder if I need to file a sexual harassment claim." He winked as he placed the pen back on my desk near my hand. He was close. So close, I could feel the heat of his skin rising to meet me.

It was at just that moment I realized the angle of the glass door reflected exactly what I had been looking at.

Thank the Goddess he didn't stick around long enough for me to respond. Carter sauntered out the door with that big white smile beaming from ear to ear.

Get your shit together, woman. Time to get your head in the game.

I lost the case.

Melanie Price's rich daddy only wanted custody to get back at the mother. His ultimate coup de grâce was severing their ties altogether. I don't know who he bribed, but he got full custody.

I consoled my client, who was currently reduced to a puddle of tears. She clung to me in desperation. She looked so pathetic, it was hard not to glare back at her ex-husband with the stankiest stank eye I could muster.

He sat smirking like the Cheshire Cat as he dragged Melanie off with him. The giant a-hole didn't even bother to look at his own daughter because he was too busy gloating over his victory and relishing the pain of his now completely bereft ex.

Melanie screamed like a wounded cat as she made a last-ditch effort to pull away and run back to her mother.

She was a feisty one. Almost broke free.

Almost.

Unfortunately, Melanie's attempts were in vain. Her father was too quick for her. She was going to get a bruise the way he manhandled her. I almost hissed.

I pressed my lips together, clamping them tight, biting down on them to keep from showing any emotion. Baring my teeth and hissing at someone after losing a case? No matter how foul a creature that man was, that was totally beneath me and bizarre as all get-out.

What the hell is wrong with me?

I'd never been anything other than calm, cool, and collected in a courtroom, from the time I set foot into the building until I got back to my car.

There were no tears, no anger, no genuine emotions.

Whatever emotions I showed were fabricated, controlled, like an actor in a play. If I needed the jury to be sympathetic, I wore one face. If I wanted them to be angry, I wore another.

None of them were the real me.

In this particular moment, after this particular trial, something snapped.

The clear, firm line between the real me and the court me had been severed.

"We'll file an appeal, Susan. We'll do everything we can to get her back."

"I can't pay. I'm broke, Amira." The words rushed out in a frenzy of pain before she let out a mournful wail that crushed my soul.

Her ex-husband stood by the door with his back pressed against the doorjamb, soaking in the warm rays of her agony. A wicked grin on his lips twitched as he clutched the struggling eight-year-old beside him with an iron grip.

"Rich fucker got away with it...again."

Shit!

I hadn't meant to say anything out loud.

What is going on with me? I have to get out of here. Now!

Just had to hold it together long enough to get Susan to a state where she could leave the room.

"Do you need someone to take you home?" The question hung in the air. I put up a temporary facade of composure. My words weren't warm and comforting as normal.

She got the hint.

Susan backed up after giving me one last squeeze. She wiped her eyes with the sleeves of her shirt as we'd long ago run out of tissues.

"No, Jason will drive me." She waved her hand in the general direction of the gallery. I saw a small balding man with tiny ferret eyes staring at us from a worn wooden bench.

The dude had given me the creeps the entire time we were in trial.

She was a grown-assed woman who had just lost custody of her daughter. I didn't think this was the best time to tell her to watch out for the unsettling rodent of a man who I'm pretty sure didn't have the best of intentions toward her.

Perhaps it was a pattern, shacking up with guys who weren't good for her. Maybe she was wired to not look out for her own best interests.

She was the complete opposite of me in so many ways: a mother, no college education, not an orphan. We might both be broken, but I chose to avoid all relationships. Life was hard enough without added distractions.

My career always had and always would come before a man.

Chapter Six

Florebelle

Mrs. Pettigrew's office was bizarre to say the least. There were taxidermy animals as far as the eye could see. Disconcerting. Not something most people would feel comfortable being surrounded by in their therapist's office. There was nothing to do but roll with it. Especially with a recommendation from Mrs. Spigot. She trusted her implicitly. After all, it's pretty hard not to trust someone who's made a part-time job out of saving your hide.

Florebelle settled into the cheap black bucket seat. It reminded her of old-school Ikea chairs. Its simplistic design lacked any sense of flair or style apart from its sweeping curves, giving a false presentation of comfort. After sitting in it for less than five minutes, her butt hurt. Her tailbone throbbed as the unforgiving plastic cupped her in all the wrong places.

Any attempt at sitting still without squirming failed miserably. She was afraid if this Mrs. Pettigrew woman caught her fidgeting too much, she might be inclined to think Florebelle was up to something.

In an attempt to distract herself from the rapidly increasing butt pain, she looked around the room and noted several other decorations besides the super-creepy taxidermy "art." None of those objects were any more reassuring or comforting, though. A few books lay scattered around as if someone had hastily set them there as a pretense of normalcy.

She wondered if a visit to the optometrist might be in order soon. She was getting older. Maybe she needed a new prescription, because the names of the books were fuzzy and illegible.

Florebelle couldn't read a single title. After a moment of reflection, she couldn't recall having any similar issues in the recent past.

Maybe it's one of those things that sneaks up on you? You don't notice it until one day you do.

She sighed. After all the weird things she'd been dealing with, having something so simple as the need for a new pair of glasses was pretty darned refreshing.

A relatively safe magazine lay half open on the fiberboard coffee table directly in front of her. She scooped it up, hoping it wasn't covered in stranger-kid germs or worse—boogers—because it was some Nat Geo Kids-type thing, only the generic version.

She flipped to page twenty-three, which was the shortest, lamest article about giraffes she'd ever seen. After getting about three paragraphs in, she heard someone clearing their throat.

Holy shit, she's tall!

Tall and skeletal. Florebelle wondered how long the poor woman had for this world. She looked like a frigging skeleton trying to act as human as possible to fool other actual humans and was failing miserably at the pretense—much like the magazines scattered about the waiting area.

The oversized black dress didn't hide her bony joints very well either. Though the woman was doing everything she could to soften the edges, she was all hard, jutting angles topped off by a thick mop of what could only be described as a beige upended broom atop her head.

Florebelle was rendered speechless. Lord only knew what the look on her face was like as she scanned Mrs. Pettigrew's body like a lecherous pervy dude in a bar before last call.

Her face...

It was framed by unruly hair and looked like dry parchment had been stretched over a human skull by a child with ADHD trying to half-assedly finish a homework assignment so they could get back to playing video games.

The thought suddenly struck her that the woman standing there was a grotesque human version of one of the stuffed animals on the wall. There were only two key differences: she was a walking, and presumably talking, caricature of a human.

"Damnable true sight," Mrs. Pettigrew whispered under her breath before literally cracking into a sarcastic smirk. The deep furrow of lines branching out from her slit of a mouth caused the lopsided smile to shatter her face like a fractured ceramic sculpture. A face tenaciously held together by nothing more than Elmer's glue and dreams. "Florebelle Fairfield?"

She nodded slowly, not taking her eyes off Mrs. Pettigrew's face because she was afraid she'd have to pick up the pieces as it crumbled to dust on the floor.

Mrs. Pettigrew swept her bony arm in front of her, gesturing toward the hallway she'd presumably just come from. There was a ballerina's grace to the motion. Florebelle expected her movements to be on the herky-jerky side, reminiscent of an effect in a horror movie. "Right this way, please."

Jareth

"The Five Laws?" Florebelle asked from the main entrance to the Witch's House.

She'd been chatting with Mrs. Spigot for a few minutes, and it sounded like the older witch might have a solution for Florebelle's night terrors. Up till this moment, Jareth had been completely unsure what to do, rendered powerless and depressed because he wanted nothing more than to bring back the bright, spirited woman he'd first met on that train just a few weeks ago.

Lately, she'd been an absolute wreck from a complicated slew of emotions he wasn't able to deal with. Their relationship was new and their cultures so vastly different, it was almost impossible to know what to say or do when these situations occurred. And they'd been popping up more and more frequently of late.

Florebelle's nightmares particularly concerned him. He knew little about human dreams in general, but she was half fairy, and he'd never witnessed any of his kind so deeply traumatized that their dreams resulted in physical altercations.

He'd been hiding the bruises for several days.

If she'd seen the aftermath of what she'd done, he didn't think she'd ever be able to forgive herself. For all her toughness, she was sensitive when it came to her actions hurting others. It was a quality he admired about her.

The fae weren't usually built that way. Whether that was because of necessity or culture, he wasn't sure.

She'd scratched through his newly healed wounds last night. They weren't mending as fast as they normally would, likely because of their link and her lineage.

When someone from the royal line inflicted damage, it would often heal slowly.

Who knew what other powers might manifest in her? And Goddess help them if anything happened while she was sleeping.

She had little experience with magicks in general and even less control over her own, everything being so new, but her powers would grow with each passing day now that she'd been in contact with the bloodstone ring.

He heard her footsteps receding down the hallway, then heading up the stairs.

Jareth's face fell as he thought about her moving her belongings to the Rose Room. How he wished her friends had stayed longer in Orphic Cove. He had a feeling they would be back soon. Perhaps they could help with this mess he wasn't equipped to handle. There was another feeling he hadn't been able to shake. A knot in the bottom of his stomach that something terrible was about to happen.

Something well outside anything he could control.

That neither of them could control.

He scratched at his left arm, temporarily forgetting the itch was because of healing. The fragile skin broke open yet again and bled through his shirt, turning the black fabric several shades darker.

At this rate, he was going to have to head back to the fae realm and take a dip in one of the healing pools.

With the queen of the Seelie Court out for Florebelle's head, he couldn't afford to be in anything other than tiptop shape. Newly healed from the severe burns covering his entire body after a brief imprisonment in a silver box, tossed into the garbage pits of the Unsanctified Lands, Jareth was lucky to be alive.

That wasn't his chief priority.

Currently, his sole responsibility was protecting Florebelle.

Whether that came as a direct order from his queen or not, it was what his heart told him to do. Protecting her didn't just mean making sure she didn't come to any physical harm. It also meant ensuring her mind stayed in one piece.

He respected Mrs. Spigot, but wasn't sure sending Florebelle off to see Mrs. Pettigrew was the best choice. Her practice, term used loosely, held a high chance of leaving her patients worse off than when she'd started.

The front door closed.

How long have I been standing here?

He realized Florebelle had just left for her appointment and decided it was in her best interest to follow her.

Straight to Mrs. Pettigrew's lair.

He stepped into the nearest shadow and vanished.

Florebelle

She couldn't keep her eyes off the woman. No matter how rude she knew she was being, Florebelle just couldn't stop staring.

Mrs. Pettigrew led her back to the office down a long, uninteresting corridor enclosed by yellowing white walls, bare except for one random picture frame containing a butterfly wing larger than any butterfly she'd ever seen.

The hallway smelled of old newspapers and dust. Her

nose tickled, but she held off the sneeze through pure determination.

It didn't feel right to break the silence.

Maybe that's not dust. Maybe that's just what she smells like.

Florebelle immediately chastised herself for thinking the emaciated woman looked like she'd smell—of dust and antique books—as if the patina of old age left a discernible odor.

How rude am I? My mother taught me better than this!

They were about to pass through the open door at the end of the hallway. She felt like she was being led to her own destruction.

Her anxiety rose with each step and her heart jumped up into her throat, making it even harder to breathe.

If this keeps up, I'm going to hyperventilate and pass out before I even make it to the couch.

Mrs. Pettigrew stepped aside just before passing through the doorway, extending a hand and bidding Florebelle to enter.

She stopped to examine the woman's ancient visage more closely.

In the light, she looked completely different.

What the hell, I must be losing it! Is this a figment of my imagination or some kind of magickal spell?

The gaunt woman who had looked like she'd been unceremoniously shoved into an ill-fitting human-body costume was now statuesque. Her cavernous cheeks were full, plump, and pink. Her sunken lips and eye sockets were those of a twenty-year-old.

Florebelle walked past her into the room confused and, however impossible it might seem, even more speechless than before.

"Please, sit down."

Even her voice was different—more youthful and fresh.

It was alluring, at least a half octave higher than before. That change made it pleasant enough to be almost hypnotic.

She felt her anxiety melt away and realized she'd already made her way onto the soft brown leather couch directly across from the transformed Mrs. Pettigrew.

Florebelle didn't even remember walking this far into the room and definitely had no recollection of sitting down.

With hands folded neatly in her lap, she waited, unsure how to proceed.

The awkward silence stretched on.

Am I supposed to go first? Is she trying to get me to fill the silence with deep, heartfelt confessions? Maybe she's just observing me and how I react to uncomfortable situations. Or perhaps I'm thinking too hard about the whole thing and letting my ADHD make my mind wander off in about fifty different directions?

She felt so damned sleepy. The couch was way too comfy.

"So, tell me a bit about why you're here, Florebelle."

Ugh. She went straight for the goods. I was secretly hoping we'd ease into it. Talk a bit, try to make me feel comfortable but, nope. Mrs. Pettigrew went straight for the jugular.

"Well, this is all super new and my mind still hasn't wrapped around the whole concept of magicks and fairies, but apparently, I'm the heir to the Seelie Court. My ex-boyfriend is my unrelated brother by marriage, and I'm pretty sure the queen is out to get me. Well, kill me, I mean."

She peeked furtively at Mrs. Pettigrew to gauge her reaction, but the older/mysteriously younger woman just sat quietly, waiting for Florebelle to continue.

"I don't know how to process all this. Plus, I moved in with a fae guy from the Unseelie Court with no job or way to pay my bills, and I'm not sure if that was the right decision. I'm scared and confused and, frankly, wondering if I've lost my frigging mind."

Why did I say all that? I don't even know this woman and I just blurted out things I've never even fully admitted to myself.

And yet, Mrs. Pettigrew just sat there, continuing to stare without even subtly acknowledging Florebelle had said a single word.

"Is there something else you're looking for? I don't know how this works."

Mrs. Pettigrew smiled and continued observing with an inscrutable look on her dewy, fresh face.

Is she satisfied? Did I fail some kind of test?

The more Florebelle questioned things, the more tired she became. It was increasingly difficult to keep her eyes open, and the edges of the room were becoming blurry as her tunnel vision focused on Mrs. Pettigrew...and Mrs. Pettigrew alone.

"I've also been having horrible nightmares. I'm tied up, falling into a bottomless pit. Being consumed by some invisible monster. Pretty sure it means something, but I got my degree in computer science, not dream analysis."

She yawned and settled back, relaxing into the velvety feel of pliable, worn leather. The cushions wrapped around her like the hug of a lover. Her head lolled to the side, and she jerked awake with a full body spasm.

What's happening to me?

It was as if she had sudden-onset narcolepsy induced by the ultracomfortable therapist's couch.

Is this woman a therapist? She's called Mrs. Pettigrew, so she definitely isn't a doctor. What do people even call therapists when referring to them by name? Wonder what her first name is...

Chapter Seven

Amira

What did I just do?

Sure, it had been an amazing night.

Our chemistry was on point, and that ass proved to be so much better unclothed in person than it had ever been in my imagination, but here I was, a forty-two-year-old woman sneaking out of a man's apartment with my high-heeled shoes clutched to my chest like a bag of precious gems.

As I tiptoed out the door, I dared to look back at Carter, sleeping like a baby in his king-sized four-poster bed. He looked like the subject of an oil painting. Some of his features softly blended into the shadows of the room, while others were made more pronounced by the pristine white linens.

They weren't so pristine anymore.

I couldn't help but smile, but the smile faltered when I realized things might be insanely awkward when we saw each other at work in a few hours.

"You look like you could use a drink."

Carter stood in the open doorway of my office, eyes full of empathy and concern.

He'd known how important that case was to me and would have heard pretty quickly through the grapevine how things hadn't gone in my favor, or he could tell from the dejected look and dead eyes. So much for my powers of compartmentalization.

I could almost feel the loss taking on a physical form, projecting like a neon sign: *Take pity on me.*

Perhaps I was waving the white flag of surrender.

Who knew?

Who knew what I was capable of in my current state of ennui?

"Yeah, I wouldn't mind a bottle or two of pinot." I tried to laugh it off, but the sound played off as tinny and fake.

Hollow.

"Well, the first bottle will be my treat." He walked to my desk, picking up a blank, errant Post-it note, playing with it idly for a few moments before lowering his voice to just above a whisper. "When I lost the Haversham case, it hit me hard. Of course, I played it off, but..." He gazed out the tinted window into the darkness outside and paused to reflect. "Sometimes, it's nice to have a friend around who's felt the same pain. Even if you don't want to talk about the details. You know?"

There wasn't much else to do today. My heart wasn't in it. All I could see was Melanie being ripped from her mother, her father standing in the doorway, savoring Susan's sorrow.

Those images played through my head in rapid succession, again and again in an endless loop.

No wonder Carter could immediately tell I wasn't myself. With that kind of stuff on repeat, it's pretty damn hard to maintain a stiff upper lip. Especially since I always had a soft spot for kids.

"Marty's. Fifteen minutes." My words broke the sudden stillness of the room, too loud and too chipper to convince anyone I wasn't distressed and trying to hide it.

He gave a swift dip of his head and left without another word. I took the time to gather up the paperwork scattered across my desk like fall leaves.

That joke about a bottle or two of pinot turned into reality.

We started at Marty's, a local dive bar we frequented because it was less than a block from the office. Then we headed to the International District for a late dinner.

Sushi and dim sum always lifted my spirits. The latter was pure comfort food—carbs and meat and savory vegetables cooked to perfection. No idea how Carter knew it would be the best place to lift me out of my doldrums.

Perhaps I was giving him too much credit, and it was just dumb luck?

Either way, I appreciated the gesture as I shoved an entire ginger pork dumpling into my mouth.

"Wow, you don't mess around when it comes to dumplings. Or is this your first meal of the day?"

I laughed around the mouthful of deliciousness. Being on my best behavior had gone out the window a bottle and a half of wine ago.

In my mind, spending this time with Carter tonight wasn't a date. It was a cleansing, a way to wash away the pain of loss with tasty food, superb wine, and splendid company. It made me more open and receptive than I'd been in a long time. Especially with a man.

Usually, I was standoffish because expectations weren't something I was very fond of.

"Oh my God, you've got to try this." Carter raised his chopsticks to my lips. I closed my eyes as he slipped the dumpling into my mouth. The burst of flavor—shrimp, sesame oil, and ginger—was offset by the slight sweetness.

"Mmm, har gow!" I said after I finished savoring my bite and wiping the bit of sauce that dribbled down my chin away with a not-so-dainty dab of a napkin. "Have you ever been down the street and had their soup dumplings? They make the best in the city."

"Nope, I've only been to a couple of restaurants here. There's a great pho place nearby."

"Oh yes, they've won a ton of awards. Who needs chicken noodle soup when you have pho?"

We laughed, we ate, we drank, and we laughed some more.

With full bellies and full hearts, we paid the check and waddled out to a nearby bar to have a few more drinks.

Three hours and three times as many light rail stops later, we found ourselves outside a closed coffee shop on a random street corner. I was utterly soused and ready to catch a ride home.

"I should get home, considering we have to be back at the office in about—" I consulted my phone. The screen was blurry and unreadable through the steady drizzle of rain and my inebriation. "a few hours, I guess. Thank you for a pleasant—" I never got the chance to finish my sentence.

Carter pulled me in for a kiss.

It was bold, strong, and slightly smoky from the top-shelf whiskey he drank at the last bar, but I was totally into it. The next thing I knew, we were in his apartment, tearing off each other's clothes.

Drenched in sweat and anticipation.

"Are you sure?" he asked.

I clamped onto him like a ravenous lamprey and moaned an "mhmm" into his open mouth.

I made it home with just enough time to take a nice hot shower and turn my bedraggled hair into something that didn't tell the tale of how I'd been tossed around like a rag doll in a coworker's bed.

Anxiety crept up when I thought about seeing Carter in the office.

No, anxiety wasn't the right word. It was anticipation. I was giddy. Feeling like a schoolgirl about to go hang out with her brand-new boyfriend.

Except, we weren't dating.

It was still a pleasant feeling. Something I'd denied myself for quite some time. Pragmatic little me tried to tamp it down and go about my morning routine, but I was eagerly awaiting seeing him at the office, bright and early.

As soon as I opened my office door, I saw a paper cup of coffee from my favorite place. If my nose didn't deceive me, it was a piping-hot caramel macchiato with oat milk—darned lactose intolerance.

At first, I thought Carter had left a cheeky little note on my desk. It was right by the coffee, after all. Couldn't deny I was let down when I saw the scrap of paper was actually from my boss. He often left Post-it notes instead of just sending emails or voicemails like a normal human being.

That man could be an absolute Luddite sometimes.

C. Rm 131—9:30 a.m.

Hmmm, wonder what he wants this time. This had better be good.

I crumpled up the small yellow piece of paper and tossed it into the trash. I definitely didn't get enough sleep to deal with any weird clandestine meetings at nine thirty in the morning.

Promptness was a virtue at Bankton, Rockman, Hughes, and Wins. I sauntered up to the conference room door at nine twenty-five with my cooling coffee in hand.

When a partner wanted to meet with you, it was always best to show up early—not on time, but early. The partners themselves were almost always late, but on the sporadic occasions they weren't, and you were...?

Let's just say that rarely ended well for anyone.

Fortunately for me, I had plenty of time to sit and enjoy the rest of my brew before good old George strode in, absolutely reeking of confidence, adorned in an expensive bespoke blue suit.

Slimy little fucker eyed me up and down like a hungry dog sizing up a juicy bone left just out of reach.

"Amira, you're looking well today. All bright-eyed and bushy-tailed."

"Thank you, sir. You're looking well yourself." I almost flinched, realizing how my casual nicety might be intentionally misconstrued.

"Why, thank you." He said as he puffed his chest out. George stood in front of the door, blocking the exit. There was an uncomfortably long pause, making me wonder if I was going to be on the receiving end of bad news. The kind of news that makes the giver want to stay near the closest point of egress in case they needed to make a quick getaway. "Well, I know you're a very busy lady, so let's cut to the chase. We're considering bringing you on as partner. It's between you and Clements."

What? Partner?

Being the ambitious type, an opportunity like this was something I'd always dreamt of, but never thought possible.

First of all, I hadn't been with the company long enough to earn it. Second, I would be the first woman, a Black woman at that, to be made partner. Third, I had just lost a case.

Before I could gather my thoughts, George Wins left the room. He wasn't one for small talk, and I was sure he didn't care what I had to say on the matter, one way or the other.

The rest of the day was smooth sailing. There were no awkward moments with Carter. In fact, I didn't see him in the office at all. The only hint of him the entire day was the coffee he'd left on my desk.

I rode high on cloud nine, humming all the way home, until I stepped into my condo. Most inconveniently, I was overrun by feelings of guilt and confusion. Complicated emotions about Carter swept through me like a violent wave on a stormy sea.

Eventually, I'd have to be face-to-face with him.

Last night had been great. More than great.

It turned out to be *exactly* what I needed to get over the craptacular way I felt after losing my case and leaving poor Melanie in the clutches of her jerk-off father.

I could deal with the day-to-day failures at my job. It was naïve to think you could win every case. No one had ever accused me of being naïve. Despite the haunting images of

Melanie and the echo of her mother's sobs spontaneously blasting in my head at the most inopportune moments, I was managing just fine.

Why am I lying to myself? I need another distraction. A sexy distraction of the non-Carter variety.

The phone rang, and I just knew it was Star—my very own personal little psychic.

"Hey, I'm coming over." Her muffled voice sounded as if she was trying to block the sound with her hand so she couldn't be overheard.

"Okay. What time should I expect you?"

"How about right now?"

"You're such a dork." I pressed the button to unlock the door without even bothering to look at the monitor.

Less than two minutes later, I heard rustling and muted conversation outside my door. I smiled to myself. Star was always striking up conversations with strangers. The other residents in the building likely thought she was the actual tenant, because she spoke to them a heck of a lot more often than I ever did.

When I cracked the door to let her in, I saw she wasn't alone. I'd recognize that ass anywhere.

"Carter? What are you doing here?"

He swung around, surprised. Apparently, he'd been so deeply engrossed in his conversation with my bestie he'd completely lost track of his surroundings. That happened a lot when men talked to her.

They became absorbed by her. Engrossed to the point where everything else just melted away until she stood firmly in the center of their universe.

I'll admit it made me a teensy bit jealous, but I tamped it down right quick. Star was many things, but a home wrecker wasn't one of them, and she would never in a million years go after a man one of her friends was even remotely interested in.

"Oh, I, uh, just popped by to say congratulations. Found myself a couple of blocks away and thought I'd stop by."

"Thanks, but..." I took a beat to swallow down the apprehension and paranoia that threatened to come out in a violent assault of words. "How did you get my address?"

"You gave it to me last night. Probably don't remember because it was pretty late, and you were tired." He grinned lasciviously before wiping it away after a quick glance back at Star.

Carter had the decency to think twice about saying anything that could be remotely deconstructed to impart our actual activities.

Star winked knowingly. She'd always possessed a preternatural ability to tell when anyone had recently "had a good time," so to speak.

"Let me go drop some of this stuff off. I'll be right back," she said with a telltale impish smirk. She picked up four plastic shopping bags and walked into the apartment, promptly disappearing around a corner.

"I'm really sorry about that. I didn't know you were having a friend over."

"Neither did I. Not until about three minutes ago." I chuckled. "Star tends to do that a lot. She just kind of shows up whenever. Often happens at the most inconvenient times. I'm used to it."

"Yes, point taken. I should have called first. Anyway, I'm gonna head back home. Again, congratulations on your promotion."

"Thanks, Carter. It's not official yet. I'm actually surprised anyone's even mentioned it."

"You didn't hear? No, of course not. You left early, didn't you?" He picked at a bit of fluff on his sleeve. "John quit."

"You're saying Clements just up and quit out of the blue? That makes absolutely no sense. That man practically lived at the office."

"Yeah, we were all surprised. Swartz called me about twenty minutes ago."

Swartz was Carter's "in," a paralegal he used to work with who had all the hot goss and information no one but the upper-level executives were privy to.

"Not really sure what to say. Just found out this morning I was even in contention, and I'm not expecting any kind of formal decision for at least another two or three weeks at the earliest."

"If you're amenable to it, we can get together for a celebratory dinner tomorrow night." Carter's eyes twinkled.

He took a half step forward and leaned against the door. I was tempted to invite him in for a celebratory romp right then and there. If it hadn't been for the fresh guilt from yesterday's events and the fact Star was up to goodness knows what in my condo, I would have.

"Can I get back to you on that tonight? I need to check my schedule and see what Star's up to. That woman's like a toddler. When she's quiet for too long..." My voice trailed off as he laughed softly, making his eyes sparkle even more.

"Sure, have a great night. I'll see you in the office tomorrow, boss." He gave me a wink before turning to make his way down the hallway.

Kindly giving me yet another opportunity to view that delightful, rock-hard ass.

Chapter Eight

Jareth

"Come out, come out, wherever you are," Mrs. Pettigrew crooned from her chair.

Florebelle lay passed out cold on the couch. No doubt her somnolence was induced by the old crone. He slipped out of a shadow, appearing beside a lamp directly behind a large and ancient mahogany desk.

"Filene, up to your old games, I see."

Her bony head swiveled one hundred and eighty degrees. It was always disconcerting when she did that—body facing away from him as she eyed Jareth menacingly, as if her head were screwed on backward.

"She came to me, youngling, came to me of her own free will." Filene sneered and picked a flake of dead, dry skin off the sleeve of her oversized black dress. Her expression transformed from malice and ill intent to coy and crafty. "I can smell her scent all over you. Does Amaranth know you've been cavorting with a half-breed?"

He rolled his eyes. Amaranth was the least of his

concerns. His hand settled on the desk as a wave of intense tiredness washed over him. Jareth swayed under the weight of it all, nearly collapsing in a snoring heap beside the old desk.

"None of your shenanigans, hag!" He pressed against the rushing waves of lethargy, creating a doorway in his mind to block her control.

Stupid.

One always had to be wary in the presence of a creature such as she. Her kind were notorious for turning the tides of fate by knocking out their adversaries with minimal effort.

The door in his mind slammed shut after waging a brief, yet intense, battle with her sleep magicks.

She pouted at the loss. Her translucent, yellowing crepey skin reminded him of onion peels.

Dry, desiccated, and dusty.

"A little respect, young man. I'm several lifetimes older than you."

"Well, maybe you should act like it and stop playing games."

Jareth knew he was the one playing a dangerous game. Though she couldn't directly affect him apart from making him pass out, one word back to his queen at the Unseelie Court and he would likely pay for his insubordination in the most unpleasant of ways.

Filene, known as Mrs. Pettigrew outside the fae kingdom, was a death fae.

She'd been grandfathered into the hierarchy of the dark fae not only because of her prodigious powers and age, but because she was likely the oldest surviving member of her extremely rare race.

She was nothing more than a withered corpse traipsing around in a dying body. A body that was at least three times larger than her actual form prior to her Awakening.

He shuddered at the mere concept of death fae Awakening because it meant taking on a less corporeal guise and hijacking another living creature.

She chuckled to herself.

Her low, alluring laugh was unexpected and not altogether pleasant. She actually sounded genuine, something he wasn't used to based on his prior interactions with her and her kind.

Death fae were on the shadiest of the shady sides. Every word and movement should be held in the deepest suspicion. They were crafty manipulators, their skills honed through practice and longevity.

"Oh Jareth, you sweet young thing, I could just eat you up." She said the last three words with long pauses between each word. The way she spoke and looked at him made Jareth want to take a shower in the acid waters of Lake Hybydon.

He was sure she meant it literally. If it hadn't been for Florebelle potentially being in danger, he would just have slunk back into the shadows from whence he came, but Florebelle lying unconscious on the couch was all the incentive he needed to rustle up extra courage.

She looked tender and sweet lying there with a puddle of drool forming in the corner of her mouth. It was refreshing to see her sleeping in a state of utter peace. Ever since she'd returned from the short stint to Maryland to clear out her apartment, she'd been suffering from those wretched nightmares. It felt like an eternity had passed since he'd seen her this peaceful when her eyes were closed.

"Filene, what are you doing to her?" As he gazed at his sleeping love, his eyebrows sprang from a relaxed state to raised high in suspicion.

Filene was capable of a great many things—a few of them might be good—but that wasn't exactly what she was most

67

known for. She was a being of pure chaos. Yes, she might occasionally act in a way that was helpful for the common good, but, more often than not, she stirred up shit just to see what would float to the top.

The queen was fine with it as long as it stayed in the mortal realm or was at her own behest.

Behest, because she held no real sway over the death fae. They were never brokered into the charter that broke the Seven Lands.

"I'm doing what your queen asked me to do—looking after the half-breed girl. A service for which said queen paid a pretty penny, mind you. Her dreams, or should I say night-mares, have been induced. Seems like 'she who shall not be named' has gotten her hooks into the poor girl. I'm giving your precious charge some peace while I root out the tangles of detritus left by that psychotic little bitch, Diaphne."

"But how? How could Diaphne possibly have gotten inside Florebelle's head? The queen hasn't set foot outside the fae realm in centuries."

"You're so naïve." She tittered, swiveling her body to match the direction her head faced. Her return to a more normal position made the tension drop at least one level, though he was still on edge. "She has her ways, you tender young morsel, you."

Filene looked Jareth up and down, licking her lips as she rubbed her hands together. The dry sound of her palms sliding against each other made him involuntarily shudder with revulsion before another wave of sleepiness hit.

"For the love of the Goddess, stop trying to get inside my head."

She wedged open the door in his mind just a crack—almost an imperceptible amount. If she'd waited longer, she might have had a chance at knocking him out cold. She was back to playing her crazy game, but he could tell her heart wasn't in it. She had no genuine desire to win and was just pushing up against the edges of his boundaries to test the waters.

Filene pouted again. Her pathetic attempts at playing innocent and coy were pretty damned horrifying. She swiveled her head backward until she faced Florebelle.

"Look, if you're not going to be any fun, then let me get back to work." She held her skeletal fingers out in front of her body, which was now behind her head, and cracked her knuckles. "I don't have all day here, and these roots run deep. Steppen must have been laying the foundation for years. Tilling the field, so to speak. Do you like my gardening metaphor? Your kind typically loves that sort of thing. At any rate, I promise not to hurt her. That's what I agreed to, after all, and a death fae's word is bond."

"Is it, though?"

That wasn't something commonly heard by the rare few who survived promises made by one of her ilk.

She hissed.

A sudden chill went up his spine.

It was right then that Jareth realized she was much more powerful than he'd ever given her credit for, and calling her integrity into question, besmirching her people, might have been one step too far.

He was forcibly pushed back into the shadow he'd entered the room through, and found himself flat on his butt, back pressed firmly against a wall, with legs spread in front of him, nauseated and reeling, in the foyer of the Witch's House.

The implications of her power made Jareth's jaw drop. She'd pushed him back through the shadow world with as little effort as a feeble old woman plucking a piece of lint off her sleeve.

Remind me to never piss off a centuries-old death fairy.

Florebelle

She rarely remembered her dreams or nightmares.

This time felt different somehow. Like she was floating in a sea of calming water. Like being on an exotic vacation on some faraway beach with a mai tai in hand, complete with a brightly colored umbrella.

There wasn't even a hint of an invisible monster or an onerous sense of impending doom. The veil of dread had been lifted—taken away—and she was left relaxed, almost to the point of boredom.

Mrs. Pettigrew was milling about in her mind. Florebelle wasn't sure how she knew this, but her brain felt like someone foreign was there, sifting through her thoughts and allowing them to slide back down, similar to a kid letting sand flow through their fingers on the beach.

No. It's more like a chef draining pasta in a colander.

Mrs. Pettigrew touched some tender part of her that hurt, then tugged that fragment up from the hole it was blocking in the colander. Each pulled strand became untangled from the massive pile of "pasta." When the process was complete, she was left feeling calm and relaxed, more happy and at peace with herself and the world than she had in weeks.

This is better than a day at the beach sipping umbrella drinks!

Again, she had absolutely no idea what was going on, but the relief it brought caused her to accept it without question. Deep down, she knew she'd wonder why she was so cool with the whole thing, but for the moment, Florebelle chose to just go with the flow.

Everything was going swimmingly. She was sitting on the beach in a nice, comfy lounge chair. The warm sun beat down on her body. She was loose and carefree, the same way she'd felt after her last visit to the masseuse. The mai tai she occasionally sipped paired well with the stunning view as she gazed out at the serene, calming waters of the horizon.

Everything was going great until she felt herself being dragged along by one of those errant spaghetti strands. She could almost feel Mrs. Pettigrew's wizened fingers grabbing at an exceptionally slippery piece that was black and rotten.

The bad strand wound itself through the whole batch, hiding in the mass's core. She sensed it was burying itself deep in the center of her subconscious, like a snake going to ground.

"Well, look at what I found here." Mrs. Pettigrew barked her laughter, sounding the same as that of a barking seal. The force of the sound bombarded Florebelle from all sides, crashing against her from every direction all at once. The sensation weakened her.

It felt like a drain being pulled out after surgery. A sucking snake, wet and warm, and so comfortable inside you that when it's pulled free, it makes you want to vomit.

Please make it stop!

Mrs. Pettigrew yanked and yanked on the insidious black strand. Florebelle's once happy dream transmogrified into a nightmare. Though still nowhere near as bad as the others, it was still traumatizing.

Especially since she had no control whatsoever over what was going on.

All she knew was that the therapist was pulling out some fetid, evil thing that had burrowed deep inside her. Then...

Relief!

It was instantaneous and so intense, her entire body relaxed into a blissful heap. Not a feeling she was accustomed to when asleep, because in the dreamscape, one's physical body was always an imagined version, never the real thing.

She fell even deeper into the comfy brown leather couch, falling so deeply into the caress of soft, brown fabric and springy cushions that she wondered if she were going straight through to the other side.

Florebelle opened her eyes.

"I couldn't get it all. Diaphne left a nasty little surprise inside you, my dear." Mrs. Pettigrew's speech was stilted and abrupt, punctuated by smacking sounds. Florebelle was horrified by the sight of the woman chewing hungrily.

Do my groggy eyes deceive me? Did she just suck up the last bit of a noodle that held a disturbing resemblance to gray matter? Nope! I'm not even going to think about that.

Curiosity got the better of her, and she couldn't contain herself. "Do I want to know what you're talking about?" she asked, perhaps a bit more defiantly than she should have.

"I wasn't able to get it all out. The taint wiggled its way through your natural defenses and got in deep. I'll likely need several more feedings..." She sniggered to herself before continuing, "Several more *sessions* before we're able to rid you of it completely. Until then, you're pretty much a sitting duck for Diaphne."

"A sitting duck? What's that supposed to mean?"

"It means she's likely going to attempt to kill you, ruin your life and mental health, aka—drive you completely insane using fear, paranoia, and hysteria, all born of a lack of sleep. At least until I can eradicate the stain. Never seen anything like this before." Mrs. Pettigrew grew pensive, eyes half-lidded before shaking her head as if to clear it. "No, it can't be that," she said under her breath.

"Can't be what?"

"Nothing, nothing at all. Don't worry your pretty little head about it." She rocked back and belly laughed. After she regained her composure and took a few steadying breaths, her mirth turned to mild annoyance. "Okay, you can go now. I need a nap."

Mrs. Pettigrew belched and rubbed her emaciated stomach, causing the black fabric of her tent of a dress to show exactly how gaunt she was. Except for what appeared to be a newly formed food baby.

Exactly how much of that thing inside me did she eat?

"Oh, indigestion. Haven't had that for a while." She let out another burp. This one wasn't nearly as loud and obnoxious as the last.

Florebelle reclined on the brown sofa in disbelief. This was not at all how she'd expected this appointment to go. How naïve of her to think she'd come to a therapist and, you know, talk. Perhaps get a few exercises or a referral for a psychiatrist who'd prescribe her some meds.

Nope, she ended up falling asleep on a couch with some creepy old/young woman eating tainted worms she'd pulled out of Florebelle's sleeping brain.

I guess it's just another day in Orphic Cove.

Chapter Nine

Amira

I found Star hanging out in my craft room. Apparently, the bags she'd brought with her were filled to the brim with yarn.

"Where'd you get all that?"

"Oh, the lady next door to me passed away. Her son saw me coming home and asked if I wanted to take my pick of her craft supplies. Poor little lamb looked so lost. I mostly went in to console him, but when I saw ninety percent of her craft supplies were yarn, I thought I'd grab a few skeens for you."

"Skeins," I said absently.

"Skeins," Star repeated. "You know I'm not going to remember that."

She opened the last bag and placed several fluffy blue wool balls beside several fluffy blue alpaca balls. Her heart was in the right place, but she had no idea how the yarns were arranged. I'd have to go through and organize things later.

I loved Star to pieces, but she often wound up making more work for others when she "helped."

"Well, thank you for enabling me."

She laughed as she slid the last ball of yarn in place. "I know. I know, but I couldn't resist. It felt like they all needed to go to a good home."

"I welcome you and your feelings any time there's yarn involved. Bring it on!"

I walked over to pick up the empty bags scattered on the floor.

"So, did you bang that hot guy last night, or what?"

"Jesus, Star. You don't mess around, do you?"

"Come on. I can practically smell him on you. And he's built like a brick house. The dude made my panties wet. I'd have pounced if I didn't know he had a thing for you."

I rolled my eyes. "Come on. He does not have a thing for me. Even if he did, you know it wouldn't work out."

"I'm so sick of that shit, Mimi. You deserve love. We all do. And being with a guy doesn't necessarily mean you have to marry him and have kids. It could just be a fun little fling."

I raised my eyebrows at this one. Flings were Star's domain. She was the most sexually secure creature I'd ever met. She did *who* she wanted *when* she wanted. There was no guilt or shame in her game.

Florebelle and I weren't made of the same stuff as Star, though I had to admit sometimes I wish I were.

"Yeah, okay. Let's shelve this conversation and figure out dinner. I'm going to head down to the gym, then take a shower, which means you'll have to entertain yourself for about an hour."

"You and your damned routines. Can't you chill out on a Wednesday night when one of your best friends is in need?"

"In need?" I asked suspiciously.

"Well, I need you!" She lunged forward and wrapped her

arms around me. I was caught up in a rather enthusiastic bear hug I couldn't help but return.

"I love you, Starlet."

"Love you too, Mimi-bear." She held me close for another second before putting her hands on my shoulders and pushing me back at arm's length. "Now go work out while I rifle through your clothes. We're going somewhere fancy tonight. My treat."

"Oh, is this a surprise? Color me intrigued."

———

I was impressed.

When Star brought me to the restaurant, I was anything but. A ramshackle building way too close to the "bad side of town." It looked more like a flop house than the kind of place someone went to for a good meal. Perhaps that was part of the allure. Regardless, my shock was apparent when we set foot inside, despite my protestations and asking about fifty times if she was sure she wouldn't like to go somewhere else. Somewhere...nicer.

The glass chandeliers tinkled in a way that only Swarovski crystals can. They reminded me of icicles in the coldest parts of winter. The crispness of the very air seemed to make the refracted light gleam off them in sharp, clearly defined prisms of light. The rest of the interior was dark wood and blue velvet.

In any other capacity, I might have considered the ostentatious nature to be stuffy and antiquated, but somehow, it was pure elegance. It gave an inviting sense of warmth while also providing a regal opulence. The enticing aromas wafting through the air made my mouth water in a most unbecoming way.

Suddenly, I couldn't wait to be seated at this restaurant and dig into what was sure to be a scrumptious meal.

It reminded me of the Witch's House back in Orphic Cove. Completely different aesthetic, but the wonderment and excitement, along with the warm, comfy feelings, brought back fond memories of eating sumptuous meals with my besties.

"Table for two," Star said to the hostess, who was dressed in a black chiffon cocktail dress that was leagues above what I was used to restaurant employees wearing. The woman looked like she was about to go to a fancy dinner party or an upscale charity event.

I looked around and saw almost everyone else at the restaurant was outfitted in a similar fashion. Star and I were severely underdressed. We looked cute, and our outfits were fine for a night out in a regular upscale place, but this was next level.

"Um, Star?" I muttered under my breath, trying not to draw the attention of the hostess.

"Name under the reservation?" The hostess didn't even look up. For that, I was grateful, but there was absolutely no way she was going to let us in.

"Please tell Alexandre that Star Maloney's here.

The hostess finally focused on us, her eyes not so casually scanning up and down our respective bodies.

There it was—the twitch of a sneer she was not so carefully attempting to hold back.

"Okay," she said slowly, her voice rife with derision. "If you'll please wait a moment, I'll notify Mr. Alexandre."

This was embarrassing. Her words were polite, but her tone? Pure sarcasm. After her initial perusal, her eyes didn't even flit in our general direction again. I swear I heard her laugh when she turned and made her way through the swinging doors I assumed led to the kitchen.

She returned a few minutes later, cheeks pale, hands on her stomach as if she were holding back a bout of nausea.

"If you'll please follow me. I'll take you through to Mr. Alexandre's private dining room." The timidity and subservience in her voice was confusing and made me highly suspicious, but we followed her through the dining room, amid the stares of diners.

I sensed their disbelief when they saw us being led through the doors.

I had a feeling this wasn't normal, but then, how often did you see guests taken back to the kitchen of a restaurant?

They probably thought we were new hires or something. Especially with the way we were dressed.

The opulence of the main dining room had nothing on Mr. Alexandre's private dining room. It must have been a bitch to keep maintained! Everything was white or made of crystal.

It was almost too bright for me to see, so crisp and clean and pure.

Not a single drop of sauce on the tablecloths. Everything was immaculate to the point of being almost virginal. The merlot in his glass made a counterpoint, so stark red, it looked like a glass of blood.

"Star, my dearest," he said in a deep, commanding baritone. His French accent had me feeling a bit tingly and anticipatory.

Mr. Alexandre simply oozed sex appeal.

He wiped his mouth with a dazzlingly white napkin and stood. Alexandre was a tall drink of water with salt-and-pepper hair and a neatly trimmed beard. His shoulders made me think linebacker, but his hips made me think dancer. The tuxedo he wore clung to every muscle and showed him off to the best advantage.

Before I had a chance to finish my hungry stare, Star jumped into his arms and stuck her tongue so far down his throat, I half expected him to cough and beg for the Heimlich maneuver.

Instead, he returned her kiss with twice as much ardor.

I turned away, unsure of where to look. This was intense. I'd been around Star and her lovers before, but I didn't know where to go if the rating got higher than PG-13.

"Sorry, Amira. I haven't seen my Alex for about three months. The best kisser on both sides of the Atlantic."

They both laughed, gazing into each other's eyes with a burning intensity that made me afraid they were about to go at it again. Next time...with fewer clothes.

"I was wondering if I'd see you again. So happy you took me up on visiting my little restaurant. How did you know I was back in town?" Alexandre sat down with Star in his lap.

"I could sense it." Star daintily picked a piece of meat off his plate with her fingers and popped it into his mouth just past his lips. She pushed it in slightly with her pointer finger. As she slid her finger deeper into his mouth, he sucked on it.

They both possessed a carnal ravenousness I knew wouldn't be denied.

"Umm, I think I'm going to go to the little girls' room." My voice was higher than normal. Almost squeaky.

I backed up toward the doorway we'd just come through as quickly as possible, with no idea where the bathroom was. Didn't really care, I was just using it as an excuse to get the hell out of there before I saw something I could never unsee.

Didn't need those images permanently seared into my brain.

I walked through the dining room so fast, it was impossible to register if anyone was staring at me this time. In my haste to get away, I realized I didn't know how long I should take to ensure my arriving safely when they were done getting "reac-climatized" with each other after their three months apart.

The cool night air stung as it hit my bare skin. I took a deep breath. Funny how I didn't realize I had been holding it since I ran out of that room. Holding my breath that long took me back to my childhood.

"Amira, Amira," Star practically screamed as she ran up behind me. "Show Florebelle how long you can hold your breath."

I turned to face them both, confused by the request.

"Okay, hold on." Star fished out her stopwatch. She turned to make sure Flo was watching. "Go." She clicked to start the timer as soon as I inhaled deeply.

Seconds turned to minutes before I felt the slightest need to take a breath.

I tapped out more because of the way they were looking at me than from the need for oxygen. I could hear the click of the stopwatch stopping when I exhaled and waited expectantly for her to read the time off so we could get on to bigger and better things.

"Six minutes and forty-seven seconds," she whispered,

looking back at Florebelle with wide eyes. Florebelle looked between the two of us, disbelief and confusion in her eyes.

"Ouch," I said, my reverie broken. Someone clipped my shoulder as they walked out the door. The door I had rudely stopped right in front of and blocked.

"Sorry." The hostess's coat lay draped across her arm, and her eyes widened in abject fear when she recognized me. "Oh God. It's you. I'm so sorry. Please don't tell Monsieur Peppard. He'll have my head." She looked like she was about to burst into tears. Her free hand went up to her neck as if to shield it. She stumbled before hurrying down the street at a near run.

What the hell?

Chapter Ten

Florebelle

S he woke up feeling all kinds of warm, cozy, blissful, and well rested, something she hadn't experienced in far too long. It was so nice to get a full night's sleep, it made it difficult to get out of bed.

How many days has it been since I last slept through the night?

Florebelle couldn't recall the last time she hadn't been awakened by a nightmare. On the cusp of falling back asleep, she jerked awake and dragged herself out of the comfy bed, reluctant to start her day.

She felt the anticipation of a long, lush shower and grinned at the thought of slathering herself in Star's home-made bodywash and shampoo, immediately followed by a scrumptious breakfast alone in the main dining room.

Eating down here always felt awkward since she wasn't a paying guest. Mrs. Spigot wouldn't accept anything in the form of compensation besides the odd compliment. Florebelle had no idea how the woman kept the place running as there never really seemed to be enough guests to pay for upkeep.

How the heck does she even keep the lights on? I haven't seen anyone in at least two weeks, and the one guy who shuffled through only stayed for one night!

With a satisfied belly pat, she toddled off in search of Jareth. The only way this morning could be any better would be to have her man at her side.

All felt right with the world, and she was quite ready to take full advantage of her newfound happiness. The way she'd been acting, she was hell-bent on giving Jareth a dose of a nongrumpy version of herself. Time for both of them to simply enjoy each other's company.

Plus, she was eternally grateful to just feel like herself again. So grateful, she wasn't keen on going about her day like it was just any old, normal, boring one.

She wanted to do something fun and surround herself with people she absolutely loved spending time with. Since her besties were currently on the other side of the continent, she figured she'd pour all her happy into her boo.

It took a little wandering to find him. Jareth sat in the overstuffed chair closest to the reception desk, reading a day-old newspaper. She snuck up behind him and planted a kiss on the back of his neck.

He acted surprised, but she was certain he knew precisely where she was at all times. She wasn't as stealthy as him, and Jareth possessed a preternatural internal Florebelle GPS system.

His eerie acuity had creeped her out on more than one occasion.

"How would you like to go to the fae realm today?"

Her eyebrows shot up in surprise. She was rendered

temporarily speechless. The invitation came as quite a shock to her system because it sprang out of nowhere.

"Sure, I'd love to!" Her quizzical look receded and she broke out into a big, beaming grin as she wrapped her arms around Jareth's neck.

She would more than love to go. The stories Jareth had told her about the fairy realm were phantasmagorical, and she'd been dreaming of visiting his home. As long as she wasn't magickally appearing in the midst of danger and being dragged off by evil queens to her death.

Now that her mind headed down the dark and thorny path leading to thoughts of Queen Diaphne, she had some reservations.

"What about 'she who shall not be named'?"

Jareth gave her an impish wink. "The tree in the woods is the path to the Seelie Court. There's a completely different route to where our lands lie. We won't have to worry about Diaphne. Her influence doesn't extend to the Unseelie Court. Unfortunately, that doesn't mean things are completely safe."

"I'm almost afraid to ask what that's supposed to mean. Hopefully, you're not being intentionally cryptic on my account?"

"Well..." He hesitated. She could tell he was taking time to form an explanation that wouldn't upset her. "There's some tension between a couple of tribes, but my understanding is that things have settled down at the moment. There's something I need to do for the queen, and I thought it was safe enough to take you with me."

"As long as you think it's safe." Florebelle tensed. Something else was going on. She couldn't put her finger on it, but she had a sneaking suspicion warring tribes weren't Jareth's only concern. Instead of pressing the issue, she made a conscious effort to trust him.

After what she'd gone through with Steppen, placing trust in fae men didn't come easily.

"Wonderful! We'll leave this afternoon."

She turned to walk away before realizing she hadn't asked the most obvious question. "How long should I pack for?"

Jareth was confused. "Pack?"

"Yes, I have to bring clothes and beauty supplies, a tooth-brush. You know? How long will we be there? Time doesn't seem to work the same way there as it does in the mortal realm."

"You won't need to pack anything. We'll be in the queen's court. Everything we need will be provided."

Florebelle squinted at him suspiciously. "You're not some kind of prince, are you? As you know, I don't have the best track record with fae men in general, but *princes*..." Her voice faded away to silence. She couldn't finish her sentence. The wound was still too fresh.

"No, I'm not a prince or part of the royal family, as far as I know, but I get certain perks when I visit the castle."

After the last few crappy weeks they'd had together, she decided not to question him endlessly and resigned herself to sitting back and enjoying that they weren't going on just any old trip, but were heading off to the fae realm.

She was all for taking a vacation to a place full of magickal mystery and hanging with her main squeeze in his hometown.

Maybe this was the fairy equivalent of meeting the parents. A luxury she wasn't able to reciprocate. Thinking of her adoptive mother passing away almost stole her joy, but she held on tight. The sadness was just a blip in what would likely prove to be an amazing day.

Her chosen family had already met him and approved. She hadn't heard a single negative word from Star or Amira since the day they'd met him in the bowels of the fae queen's castle. She could still see that damnable woman's sharp pointy teeth glinting in the light, behind the taut lips of her wicked smile.

Florebelle shuddered at the memory.

Nope! Not today, Satan! Today's a happy day, and I intend to keep it that way through hell or high water!

"Are you okay?"

"Yeah, it's just a little chilly in here." She ran her hands up and down her arms to illustrate the point. "Speaking of which, what's the temperature like there this time of year? Should I wear a sweater? Or..."

Jareth laughed.

She loved the way his eyes crinkled up at the corners. He shook his head and brought his hands out to swoop up both of hers.

"Where we're going, it's always spring. I'm not laughing at you, by the way. It's a bit of a joke around the castle."

He pulled on her hands, swinging her around in a half circle until she lost balance and landed firmly in his lap. Jareth wrapped her up in his sturdy arms and she was instantly transported to the very first time she felt those arms around her—saving her from a nasty fall when she came hurtling out of a train bathroom in full panic mode.

Jareth's nose nuzzled up behind her ear. His warm breath tickled the back of her neck, making her feel a sudden tingle of anticipation. The pillow-soft caress of his lips pressed against the exposed flesh at her nape.

Florebelle's breath quickened, as did her pulse. She eased into the sensation, closing her eyes and leaning back to press her body more firmly against his.

A throat cleared.

"Ahem."

Florebelle's eyes flew opened as she jerked away from

Jareth, nearly causing them both to tumble forward out of the chair. She felt like a teenager getting caught by her parents making out with her boyfriend.

"Aren't you two precious?" Mrs. Spigot announced as she clapped her hands together and veritably cooed at them adoringly.

Florebelle's cheeks grew hotter by the second. They'd been about to get busy in the main reception area.

OMG. Self-control much?!

Florebelle took the opportunity to dash out of the room and rush upstairs to grab a few things despite being told she didn't need to. She really wasn't sure what "everything would be provided" actually meant.

Do they have tampons and menstrual cups in fairyland, or do you just shove a daisy up your wahoo and pray? Heck, what are clothes even made from over there?

Sporting a bra made of leaves and a flower miniskirt held together by magicks wasn't exactly her style.

She chuckled to herself as she recalled a silly moment of dancing around her living room in her old apartment in Maryland, buckass naked. It was right before her very first trip to Orphic Cove.

She played Eve as she hid her rather large girls behind even larger monstera leaves. As much of a joke as she tried making of this whole adventure, there might be a few considerations.

Florebelle froze. She was finally going to get to know a world she not only was never aware existed until a few weeks ago, but was also an actual part of her.

A legacy stolen away for forty years. Whether she'd

reached a stage in her life where she could fully internalize it, or not—she was half fairy. It was easy enough to say the words and not truly accept the greater import of it all.

In a way, she was going home to meet her people.

She came from Seelie Court stock. The Seelie Court and Unseelie Court had been at war for decades, possibly even centuries. Visiting the Unseelie Court still meant hanging with fairies and all the other fae. It was sort of like leaving NYC and visiting your relatives in Mississippi for the first time after four decades. They might feel foreign as all get out, but they were still family. They were a part of your history and a part of your future.

She was pretty sure that wouldn't be exactly how they saw it. Her other half was human. Her ex had bitterly called her a half-breed right before she was sentenced to death. She could only assume the word carried a similarly disgusting derogatory connotation in the fae realm as it did in the mortal one.

This meeting went from just hanging out with her boyfriend and meeting the people he grew up with, to being a way for her to possibly discover some of her heritage.

A long-lost part of her culture she'd been ignorant of.

Being adopted and not having any records of her parents had always made her feel lost. Like she had no real biologically related family. Not saying her chosen family wasn't enough, but there had always been a hole she'd never had the opportunity to fill.

Now, she at least knew who her father was. That was one question answered.

Florebelle closed her eyes and sighed wistfully.

She might never get to know more about her parents since she couldn't exactly set foot in the Seelie Court without facing the wrath of Queen Diaphne—wrath that originated solely because she was born—through no fault of her own.

She set her jaw and straightened her back.

But I can still get to know more about where my father's side of the family came from. She can't steal that from me.

Her breath caught in her throat.

I'm going home.

———

"You two heading out, dear?" Mrs. Spigot stood behind the reception desk. She was obviously waiting for someone, because she rarely ever bothered to go back there unless it was to dust.

"Yes, Jareth and I are heading to the Unseelie Court. No idea when we'll be back."

"Ooh," she crooned in a way that sounded almost jealous. "You two have fun!" Mrs. Spigot gave a lascivious wink just as Florebelle heard Jareth's footsteps coming down the stairs.

Strange, he usually moved so quietly, she didn't know he was even there. He moved like a shadow.

"Off to the forest?" she asked once he made his way to her side.

"No, I have an easier method of getting to the Unseelie Court. I'm dark-fae aligned. That means no tokens or magickal words are necessary."

Jareth held his hand out toward her and bowed like a character from a period drama asking a lady to dance at the formal ball. The only thing that would have made it more perfect was if he'd clicked his heels together and flown them to their destination with fairy magicks.

Florebelle took his outstretched hand while holding back a giggle.

Instead of heading toward the door, Jareth directed her to the darkest corner of the room—between a grandfather clock and an antique china cabinet displaying floral teacups.

He walked into the shadow, and she followed him without hesitation.

Instead of thwacking into a wall, the two sauntered into a pitch-black darkness that both horrified and comforted Florebelle at the same time.

What a hell of a way to travel!

Chapter Eleven

Amira

Standing outside in the cold, I wondered when it would be safe to return to the private dining room. Hopefully, it would be soon, because I could already feel my nose reaching the point where drippage would be unavoidable.

Shivering in the chill damp, I knew I couldn't take it much longer. Afraid to go back and find those two in flagrante delicto, I scanned the street to see if there might be another restaurant I could escape to if I heard telltale signs of their activities. My stomach growled.

I was famished.

I skipped a perfectly good postworkout protein shake for this.

Things are pretty bad when you're so hangry, you reminisce about chocolate protein shakes you usually say taste like ass, just because you are stuck waiting for your friend to stop banging a guy in his private dining room.

The acrid stench of cigarette smoke wafted toward me. I

turned to cough, ready to give the inconsiderate a-hole a death glare. The inconsiderate a-hole in question was Star.

Apparently, she was done with her dirty dining room deeds and had come outside for a postcoital ciggy.

The red ember of her cigarette bobbed up and down as she rubbed her arms to keep them warm. Not sure why she bothered. I could see steam rising off her like a hot cup of coffee on a cold winter's morning. A soft puff of smoke snaked from her nostrils like the tail of a genie.

"Sorry about that," she muttered from the corner of her mouth, lips taut to keep the cigarette from falling out. "I don't know what came over me."

Star stopped trying to warm her exposed arms with the friction of her hands just long enough to pull the cigarette from her mouth and flick the ashes away from me. I was too speechless to reply. I mean, what do you say to a friend who likely just had sex with a man at the table you're supposed to now eat at?

"For the record, he did me against the wall. The table remains unscathed."

"Good to know." I rifled through my purse, hoping to find a tissue. Star pulled out a plastic-wrapped travel packet and handed it to me. "Get out of my head, woman." We laughed as I dabbed at my nose.

"Makeup check?" I turned my head from side to side so she could give me her assessment.

"Perfection. Now, let's get inside before I freeze to death."

"I'd have figured he warmed you up enough to withstand the cold of an Arctic winter."

"If you only knew, Mimi. If you only knew." With a hand on the door, she swiveled her head just long enough for me to catch a wry grin.

"Okay, let's eat."

I pushed back from the table, full to bursting. The dinner here was so fabulous, any earlier transgressions were forgiven after the first bite. I just hoped our host didn't think I had an eating disorder, because I'd consumed enough food to feed an entire football team.

Alexandre ordered for us, and we shared bites of our individual meals with each other. Never had so much fun with a stranger before at a table. Especially one who had just finished pleasuring my friend, but that awkwardness was soon lessened by the casual conversation and his magnetic charm.

Everything was going great until it was time to leave.

Then things got weird.

Nothing was said directly, but I could feel the tension in the air after we finished the last sip of coffee following our dessert. I was tired, but the vibe being given off by Alexandre left me wanting to slither out of the room. Kind of wished I had Jareth's shadow-walking capabilities right about now.

"Thank you, Alexandre. This was a most lovely evening. The food was fabulous. I can honestly say you didn't exaggerate." Star stood and stretched toward him, planting a kiss on his lips.

The room faded away to an echo, like a dream disappearing right as you wake up.

"Stay."

"I wish I could, love. But Amira and I have to head back because a certain someone gets up at the butt crack of dawn and needs her beauty rest. Plus, she's probably got some criminals to put away." She smiled back at me with love.

I wasn't altogether enamored because, after all these years, she still didn't know what I actually did for a living. This was normally when I'd chime in with something about how my specialty was family law, not criminal law.

I'd long ago come to realize lecturing her was pointless.

"Stay."

This time when he said the word, he gazed intently into her eyes. Star remained unfazed. She merely kissed him on the cheek and whispered something in his ear.

Alexandre looked shocked, perplexed, and more than a bit pissed, but his eyes softened, and he nodded in silence.

My hand reached for my water, which I gulped down nervously while Star gathered her things.

Before leaving, I turned to say a final goodbye to Alexandre, but he was gone.

Confused, I looked around the room.

"What the hell?" I muttered under my breath.

"Something wrong?" Star asked. She didn't seem remotely concerned that our host seemed to have vanished into thin air.

Guess I just didn't hear him leave.

I shook my head. "Nothing. Too much wine, I guess."

With one last look back at the seat Alexandre had occupied for the past two hours, I shrugged and made my way out to the main dining room.

"So, tell me about the guy with the nice ass?" Star asked while wriggling into one of my old college T-shirts. It was baggy on me, but she filled it out nicely.

"Nothing much to tell. Carter's a coworker."

"Was he good in bed?"

"Jesus, Star. Come on!"

"What? I'm happy for you. Positively ecstatic. And we're

best friends. Pretty sure it's in the bylaws we're supposed to talk about this kind of thing."

"Well, maybe we can talk about it more when we haven't been out until the wee hours of the morning. I need to get some sleep. Five a.m. comes pretty damned early. You know?"

"Look," Star said as she grabbed my arm and pulled me close. "You deserve to be happy, and this guy obviously makes you ecstatic. More than once, judging from the way you were walking. Why not just enjoy it for what it is? Not like he's asked you to marry him."

I tried to think of a way to distract her, but I was too tired. Letting her say her piece was the path of least resistance. She'd say what she wanted to say, then we could bid each other good night, and I could hit the sack.

The annoyed sigh escaped involuntarily.

"Fine. I'll shut up. I'm just saying that enjoying a nice fling is a pleasure in and of itself. And we all deserve a little pleasure now and again."

"Why don't you have some pleasure on me? I pick up my car tomorrow. I'll drive you to visit Alexandre every night for the next week if you lay off my sex life and leave me alone? Hmmm?"

Okay, that was uncalled for. I felt like an ass when Star bit her shaky bottom lip and dropped onto the bed, turning away from me.

Shit, did I just slut shame one of my best friends?

That was one low blow.

"I'm sorry, Star. You're right. I'm just being defensive. You didn't deserve that."

She didn't move or look at me.

This is bad.

The woman could snap back from pretty much anything.

97

I'd never seen her like this before and was starting to feel lower than dirt.

"Hey, did I tell you I'm in the running to be made partner? Apparently, the other guy in contention quit under mysterious circumstances yesterday."

My good news perked her up. Thank the Goddess.

"Oh my Goddess. Seriously?" she asked as she stood abruptly and jumped around my room like a pogo stick. "You didn't think they'd ask for another five to ten years."

"Yeah, you were right. As usual. Remind me why I don't implicitly trust you and your cards?"

"Ummmm, because you went to law school and they beat the wonder and magicks out of you with boring legal texts and bar exams?" She took three quick steps, grabbed my arms, and resumed her jumping fit.

Thank goodness she was shorter than me, or I might have been knocked out by her flying boobs.

"You're such a dork." I planted a quick kiss on her cheek at the apex of our next jump. She squealed in delight and dragged me over to the bed.

"Alexa, turn off the light."

We cuddled and chatted until it was well past the time I could reasonably think I'd be anything other than a hollow shell of a human being the next day.

"Drink this." Star handed me a horrifying gray sludge of a concoction that looked like someone had tried to turn the swamps of Florida into a smoothie.

If it had been anyone other than her, I would have thrown it in their face.

Instead, I dutifully gulped it down as fast as I could, grimacing with each reluctant swallow.

I just hoped it didn't come back up on my way to the office. I'd never thrown up in a car before and didn't plan on starting today.

By the time we pulled up to my building, the concoction had worked. I felt well rested, and my mood had improved dramatically. When I arrived at my desk, I was humming a merry tune to myself with a little bounce in my step.

It appeared I wasn't the only one. As I hummed and veritably danced through the corridors on my way to get coffee, I noticed almost everyone else was bopping around as well.

"Did you hear about John," Rosamund whispered over the lip of her ThunderCats coffee mug.

I backed away because she'd just returned from work after getting over a cold she told us was "allergies" for three days before someone from HR told her to go home.

Suffice it to say, I wasn't keen on getting too close to her.

"Clements? Yeah. I heard he quit."

Rosamund looked miffed that I already knew the latest office gossip. She recovered with a conspiratorial peek down the hallway to ensure no one was within hearing range. "He left under very suspicious circumstances."

"You don't say?"

Not one for office gossip, I usually avoided Rosamund like the plague.

Despite the fact she was always claiming allergies when she was actually spewing viral pathogens like a hydrant on the hottest summer's day, she loved to get super close and whisper her "hot goss" to anyone within hearing range. Most of the lawyers tried to steer clear of her. Perception management being what it was, you didn't want to be associated with the office rumormonger.

She patiently waited for me to go for the prompt and ask a question or show interest in her vague manipulation.

Her methods had never worked on me before, so I wondered why she thought I magickally cared now.

My assistant, Shay, popped her head around the corner. "Hey, Amira? Your client's calling and she's completely freaking out." She smirked once Rosamund started hurriedly walking away.

"You have perfect timing. Not that I'm happy one of my clients is freaking out, but the excuse was very conveniently timed indeed. I owe you one!"

Shay chuckled as I made my way toward her. She handed me a Post-it note with a hastily scribbled name and number.

"Susan Price? Are you sure?"

Shay nodded. My mirth was wiped away in an instant. "She said it had something to do with Melanie. I couldn't quite make it out with all the hysterics, but it sounded pretty serious."

"Damn."

If this had anything to do with her ex-husband, this wouldn't be good.

Chapter Twelve

Florebelle

Not only was Florebelle completely blind, but she couldn't hear anything. Instead of being afraid, she found the darkness to have a beauty and peace of its own.

Then her brain wondered if she was "fae enough" to make it through the other side of the shadow.

Will I be trapped here forever? Stuck in a pitch-black space with no beginning or end. Unable to see or hear anything. Could a person even die if they were trapped in a shadow? Or would they just exist in perpetual nothing, forever?

As the panic set in, she felt a tug and went hurtling into a room full of too much.

Too much light. Too many sounds. Too many smells.

She went from the absence of everything to complete sensory overload.

Doubled over, Florebelle did her best not to vomit or scream. Fortunately, the overwhelming barrage of external stimuli didn't last long.

"Jareth?" she heard a female voice proclaim.

A stunning blonde woman rushed toward them and wrapped her arms around him. The force of her affectionate attack unlinked their hands. He was spun around in a full circle as Florebelle stood in confusion with eyes blinking and her jaw on the floor.

"Thank the Goddess! No one would tell me where you'd gone or what had happened to you. I was afraid I'd never see you again."

The woman pushed back, holding Jareth at arm's length. She beamed at him, saying nothing for several seconds. She was clearly savoring the sight of him, saving the moment in her memory to be pulled up later like a photograph.

"You look well, but we'll have to catch up later. I'm headed off on an errand and don't have much time for pleasantries. We absolutely must have dinner tonight. So much to catch up on!"

With that, she unfurled iridescent wings, flapped twice, and launched herself straight up into the air. Right before reaching the clouds, she fluttered and performed an elegant loop, her long blonde hair flowing behind her like golden ribbons. She turned on a dime and spoke in a whisper that was as clear as if she were standing right next to them. "You should bring your friend. I've never met a mortal before."

Then off she flew. Florebelle stared after her in awe.

"Welcome to the Unseelie Court," Jareth said with a chuckle.

"She has wings?" she sputtered.

"Yes, but much like what you say to me when I try to play with your hair in public: never touch a fairy's wings."

He laughed uproariously.

"Who is she?"

"Her name is Hildesheim. Named after one of the oldest living roses in the mortal realm. She's my fiancée."

———

Florebelle was stunned into a state that transcended speechlessness.

The cavalier way Jareth just admitted he was engaged to another woman on the day he brought her here to see the sights... There was no shame in his eyes. He just smiled, scooped her hand back up, and led her down the nearest hallway as if he didn't have a care in the world.

With teeth grinding and eyes slitted, Florebelle saw red. She jerked her hand away.

"Fiancée? You're engaged?"

Jareth turned to face her with a look of surprise. She didn't know what stoked the fires more, that he didn't seem to give a shit about it, or the way his expression melted into that of a confused child.

Kind of like what happens when you explain trigonometry to an eight-year-old.

"Yes, the queen arranged the engagement right after we were born. It's not a big deal."

"Not a big deal?" Her hands curled into fists and banged into her thighs so hard, she was sure to have a bruise tomorrow. Her fingernails bit into the soft flesh of her palms. A few of the tiny crescents bled, but Florebelle didn't feel a thing.

Pulse pounding in her ears, her voice was flat, dead, and cold as ice. "Take me home. Right now."

Not only am I trapped in the fairy realm with a cheating asshole, but I've been betrayed by yet another fae. Prince or not, my track record's abysmal. This one, though? This one I truly loved. Unlike Steppen, who held me in a glamour for three years. Everything we shared was a lie.

A sudden realization hit her.

"Did you..." She caught her breath and focused long enough to get the rest of the sentence out. "Did you *glamour* me?" The last two words came out with the venom of a viper. Her words reverberated around the stone walls, bouncing gleefully down the hallway. It felt like the entire place was laughing at her.

"What? No!" His childlike innocence turned to abject horror. It was as if she'd physically slapped him upside the head.

"You swear on your...Goddess, or whatever, that you didn't glamour me?"

Jareth's skin turned red and blotchy. He took a step back. He reached toward her pleadingly.

The pain in his eyes reminded Florebelle of the way he'd looked when he was recovering from severe burns when she, Star, and Amira had dragged him from the fae realm to the mortal realm with their combined magicks.

His body had been covered in deep burns from being encased in a silver box. Each contact point seared him through—some to the bone. It was touch and go for a few days, but he'd pulled through.

Maybe I would have been better off if he hadn't.

Their trip was brief.

All in all, it lasted a little over an hour before he dragged Florebelle back through the shadow realm and landed in the foyer of the Witch's House.

The silence between them spoke volumes.

Mrs. Spigot looked up in astonishment when they popped back out from where they had left what must have been mere moments before.

She was in exactly the same place she'd been when they departed.

Her mouth opened to speak. She changed her mind and was off like a shot, not even making any excuses about folding laundry or any other bed-and-breakfast-related chore.

Florebelle stormed off to their shared room. Her teeth were clenched so hard, the muscles of her jaw had gone past quivering tension to a full-on dull ache.

Her belongings were haphazardly packed in about thirty seconds flat.

She grabbed everything she owned and tossed it all onto the bed. With her belongings piled high in its center, she snatched up the four corners of the comforter and gave one mighty tug, slinging the weight behind her. It thumped against her back, involuntarily pushing her forward several steps. She maintained the forward momentum and walked straight out the door to her room.

Once back in the safety of the floral landscape of the Rose Room, Florebelle crumpled onto the bed.

Swathed in rose-covered wallpaper and linens, hugged by the comfy mattress, and walled off from the rest of the world by the soft drape of white fabric gently cascading down each side of the four-poster bed, she sighed and let the floodgate of tears release.

There was no holding it back.

Betrayed.

First, it had been Steppen, who'd kept her enthralled and compliant for three years of her life.

He'd led her down hallways of false memories and lies that had changed her reality into a more romantic life than she'd ever led.

She was almost killed because of him and still had regular nightmares of his mother's dungeon cell, awash with guilt about unwittingly almost leading her childhood friends to their deaths because of her gaping ignorance about her past and who she was.

How could I possibly have allowed myself to fall for another fucking fairy?

All the warnings signs were there. Especially the big glaring one: a flashing red neon sign.

Why the hell would I let myself fall for another one? And this one is dark fae at that. Part of the Unseelie Court. I saw what the Seelie Court queen is capable of. Her sharp, pointy teeth glinting in the light as she sentenced my friends and me to die in a silver coffin, buried alive in a garbage pit.

Then she'd run right into the arms of the next fae male who just happened to come into her life. Maybe he wasn't as bad as Steppen, but he was close.

He made me the other woman!

Her sobs rang out, and the sounds of misery bounced off the walls, echoing back her shame.

That was one sin she'd never committed. No matter what else transpired, she'd never, ever put herself into a position to be a home-wrecker.

What kind of man cheats on his fiancée?

"He said he loved me." Her words came out in a garbled mess, full of snotty gurgles and a jaw now stiff from grinding her teeth for so long.

Everything stopped.

The tears stopped flowing, and her breath caught in her throat. Even the constant rhythmic clicking of the wooden clock hanging on the wall was silent.

The only thing that moved was Florebelle's stomach. It lurched. She felt bile rising up, coating her entire essence with its putrid, acidic sting.

I could make him pay. Pay for his betrayal of me and his fiancée. I could get vengeance for us both.

With everything in the room and inside her heart as still as death and twice as cold, Florebelle wiped the tears from her cheeks with the edge of the nearest decorative pillowcase.

Then, she slowly and methodically put away the belongings she'd retrieved from Jareth's room. She picked them up from the pile by the door where she'd rather unceremoniously dumped them.

This will require patience. Patience to plan and patience before enacting that plan.

Chapter Thirteen

Amira

I hurried back to my office, humming, playful swagger, and taste for coffee gone in an instant.

Please let Melanie be okay.

I paused when my fingertips connected with the black plastic, then steeled myself before snatching up the receiver and placing it to my ear.

"Ms. Rapaport? Oh, thank God." Susan burst into a crying jag, rendering her next few words completely unintelligible.

"Susan, I need you to take a deep breath and slow down. I can't understand what you're saying, hun." I got extremely informal when women were crying into the phone. Being all business didn't help in these situations. It took a gentler, kinder touch.

After a few false starts, she still couldn't control her breathing long enough to get anything comprehensible out and couldn't manage a full sentence before she was reduced to hysterics again.

Despite all this, because of my prodigious experience with crying women, I was able to figure out that her ex-husband was shipping their daughter, Melanie, off to a private school in Switzerland.

"Okay, Susan." People usually calmed down when they heard their names, so I made a conscious effort to repeat it as often as I could. "He sent you a written notice of intent, but we can still file an objection. If he tries to send her there before the hearing, he'll face sanctions. We have options. But you have to calm down so we can talk about this. Can you come in tomorrow?" I pulled up my calendar to check for openings while she sniffled. I could sense her nodding at her end of the line. "What about first thing in the morning? Nine a.m.?"

I'd have to rearrange a few things, but Melanie and Susan's situation affected me on a visceral level.

It would be easier for everyone concerned if she and I got together to go through her options as soon as possible. Unfortunately, today was booked solid with client interviews, consultations, and sorting through the never-ending piles of paperwork.

"Thank you so much, Ms. Rapaport. I don't know what I'd do without you."

"Happy to help, Melanie. I'll see you tomorrow. Bright and early."

With our meeting scheduled and her sniffling at least temporarily abated, I hung up the phone.

The rest of the day went swimmingly. Not a single sniffle —from employees with colds, sad clients, or any tears in sight.

It had been a long yet productive day, and I sure was glad to be back home.

Too exhausted to head to the gym after my sleepless night, I tossed my shoes into a corner and collapsed on the couch.

"Alexa, play ocean sounds."

I lay back and closed my eyes, absorbed by the sound of waves rushing up on the beach. I could almost smell the salty air and feel the sand between my toes.

Laughter.

I woke up in fight-or-flight mode, only to find Star there, giggling.

She tried to hide the sound with the back of her hand, but was failing epically.

"Sorry." She barely got the word out when she snorted again as another involuntary gale of laughter hit her. "You were snoring so loud, I was afraid someone was using a chainsaw in one of the other apartments."

"Condo," I corrected her. Drowsy, and not being the kind of person who usually wakes up in a jovial mood, it was hard not to snap at her.

I do not snore!

"Have you been here all day?" I asked instead at a clipped, measured pace.

"Yes. Just relaxing. I was going to head out but was afraid my lack of willpower would lead me back to Alexandre."

I wasn't sure what to say to that. Sometimes it was best not to say anything at all.

People often felt the need to fill the silence and would divulge more than they expected. That tactic worked particularly well on Star. She often thought out loud.

"I figured staying here would be the safest bet. Not used to people having that effect on me. The role reversal is both exciting and annoying," she said ruefully.

She didn't seem to appreciate getting a taste of her own medicine, and I didn't blame her.

Star wasn't herself when she was around that Alexandre guy.

She's never been so horny that she blew off her friends for a screw on a restaurant table—well, wall.

"You know, I forgot to mention it last night, but I bumped into the hostess and she seemed terrified of Alexandre. And it wasn't in that 'He's gonna fire me' kind of way. It was like one of my addict clients afraid they were getting sent to rehab." The last part came out without me thinking it through. "Oh, crap. Sorry. I didn't mean to imply..." My voice trailed off as I tried to think of another topic. Having this particular conversation while still half-asleep probably wasn't the best idea. "Will you stay over again tonight? I could use the company. Need to deal with a frantic client first thing in the morning before a full afternoon with Judge Shapiro."

I scowled.

Star was well aware of my deep dislike of Gwen Shapiro, and the feeling was mutual. Which meant that tomorrow afternoon was going to be an extremely stressful battle of wills.

"We'll keep it caj tonight, darling. Maybe order in some Thai and do mani-pedis?"

I was always in when Star proposed one of her infamous mani-pedi nights.

She always tossed in a foot rub, and that girl knew her way around an aching arch.

"Hell, yeah, I'm in. Should I order your usual?"

"But of course! I'll go grab the kit." She was off in a flash, swishing down the hallway to get everything set up in the guest bedroom.

How I loved a good girls' night. The only thing missing was Florebelle.

Damn, I miss that woman.

Jareth

Why is she so upset? Everything was going so well since she saw Mrs. Pettigrew. Flora was back to her old self. Or so it seemed.

Jareth was exhausted beyond measure and utterly confused. Having used up all his magickal reserves to get them to the fae realm and back in such rapid succession, it took every ounce of willpower he possessed to stay awake long enough for Flora to gather her belongings and head back to her room.

They'd been inseparable for weeks until their recent issues. The sleepless nights and occasional bouts of uncomfortable conversation were nothing compared to what had just happened.

How could Flora be so upset by my engagement to Hildesheim? Perhaps there's something more at play here than I realize, but I'm tired. So tired.

He lifted his hands to his face and saw a slight tremor.

This isn't good. Hopefully, she'll be done soon so I can lie down. Not that I want this situation to be unresolved, but I'm going to pass out for a week at this rate.

Traveling through shadows within a realm wasn't a big deal, but traveling from human to fae realm and back again with such a short period in between? That was something few fae could manage. Jareth was strong, but there would be negative repercussions.

Under normal circumstances, he could have explained it to Flora. They could have possibly stayed one night before heading back, but her rage... The look in her eyes... He was frightened. The only time he'd seen her in such a state was when they were in the Seelie Court and their lives were being threatened.

It was her strength during the moment her friends were in danger that had melted his heart and made him realize his sacrifices hadn't been in vain.

But to think of that cold, steely, hate-filled gaze being turned on him?

A shudder went through his body and wouldn't stop. He was weak and fading fast.

"Are you all right, dear? You don't look very good."

Mrs. Spigot's warm, comforting voice surprised him. Not hearing someone coming up behind him wasn't a good sign.

Jareth's body was shutting down.

"I traveled too quickly. Need sleep." His legs gave out from under him. There was barely enough time, or strength, to grab the corner of the curio cabinet he was standing next to. It kept him upright as Mrs. Spigot hurried to his side, hooked her arms underneath his armpits, and half led, half dragged Jareth to the nearest room.

The door opened of its own accord.

Florebelle

"Where the hell are you?" she whispered into the night. Her voice was a raspy hiss. Pure, unbridled hatred welled up inside her when she realized Jareth wasn't in his room. She wanted to scream in frustration until her throat was raw and bloody.

She stalked the hallway on his floor. Her eyes squinted against the barrage of feelings that boiled up inside her. Through those small slits, she saw empty room after empty room until at last—her prize.

Jareth lay asleep in a bed like an innocent child. He was curled up in a ball, shaking like a leaf. A small part of her knew that under normal circumstances, she would be concerned about his shivering.

A much larger part of her gave zero fucks.

Florebelle raised the knife.

The metal glinted in the scant moonlight bleeding around the periphery of the thick linen curtains.

Jareth

Something's not right!

His reflexes took hold of him, and he rolled over. Jareth still couldn't fully wake up. His body moved via muscle memory more so than conscious thought.

So tired.

The exhaustion and a deep chill had set deep into his bones, yet a feral part of him knew something was amiss and forced him awake despite all odds. As he opened his eyes, he saw the flash of silver stab into the mattress where his chest had been mere seconds before.

He followed the trail up the would-be murderer's arm and locked on to the face of his beloved.

"Flora? What are you doing?" His words cut through the air like a razor.

What nightmare is this?

Florebelle

My one chance for justice and the bastard ducks me in his sleep.

The scream she'd barely been holding at bay in the hallway bubbled up from her throat, and the desire for vengeance burned inside her like the fire of a thousand suns. There was only one thought in her head:

Make him pay!

Florebelle pulled the knife from the mattress and stabbed at him again.

This scream was louder. The raw power of its force clawed at the walls of her throat. She was caught in midthrust, paralyzed.

"Jareth, dear. Can you leave the room of your own accord?"

The strain in Mrs. Spigot's voice made her sound like a stranger. Her normally pleasant and cheery disposition were long gone.

She murmured a few unintelligible words as Florebelle fought against the magickal bonds. It was to no avail. Mrs. Spigot overpowered her, and Florebelle was forced onto the mattress, flat on her back with her limbs spread wide, tethered to the bedposts as if by rope.

She struggled against the invisible bonds.

Florebelle felt, rather than saw, the shadow of Mrs. Spigot as she inched closer to the bed. The invisible gag prevented Florebelle from speaking. Try though she might, all that came out were grunts.

Mrs. Spigot's sadness wrapped around Florebelle like a crown of thorns, prickly and uncomfortable. The older woman's pity was so intense, it felt as if it could make her bleed.

"My sweet girl. I'm so sorry I had to do this. Mrs. Pettigrew will be here soon. Hopefully, she can help you."

A cool cloth.

A few more murmured words.

Then sleep.

Jareth

"There's nothing I can do. She's too far gone. The only thing that can stabilize her would be her coven. They can take some of the burden and give her a few more..." Mrs. Pettigrew paused as if trying to do math in her head. "Well, it might not be worth it. At this rate, she'll be completely gone in a few days."

"Gone?" Jareth asked incredulously.

"Yes. Gone. This is a tricky little thing. Something extremely powerful triggered her recently and caused the darkness to grow exponentially," Mrs. Pettigrew replied.

"What *exactly* is going on?" Mrs. Spigot asked. She neatly tucked her knitting needles into the wicker basket beside the rocking chair she'd been planted in for the past few hours.

"She's infected. Whatever it is, it appears to eat away at the soul until the only thing that's left is a dark shell full of hate."

Mrs. Spigot's gasp pierced the silence of the room.

"This is my fault. Telling her about my engagement to

Hildesheim somehow did this to her. I don't understand. I thought she was getting better after her last visit."

"Oh, dear little innocent one. After what happened between her and Steppen, you told her she was your side-piece? If the situation weren't so dire, I'd be laughing right now." Mrs. Pettigrew shook her head and looked over Flore-belle's limp form. "Most humans believe in monogamy. And I don't know many Americans who are married off for political reasons. It's highly unlikely she understands that your marriage to Hildesheim would be in name only."

Jareth crumpled into the nearest chair. He was still exhausted from their journey, and the adrenaline that had been keeping him upright had all but run out. There was no way he'd be awake for much longer.

He needed to recover and couldn't be there for Florebelle over the next few days. He dragged himself to the bed. Gazing down, he bent to kiss her, but felt a hand on his shoulder. He turned his head to see Mrs. Pettigrew shaking hers.

"You can't touch her." Her voice was low and sad. "I'm so sorry, Jareth. I truly am."

He looked down at his beloved one last time before snatching up his phone on the nightstand beside her.

"Call Amira Rapaport."

The phone rang a few times before Amira's voice, thick with sleep, uttered a confused "Hello?"

He couldn't speak.

"Jareth? Is that you? Is something wrong? Hello?"

"It's Flora. Can you come?" His voice caught in his throat. His next inhalation was a sob.

There was a long pause before Amira answered. Her voice was much closer to normal. "Yes, I'll be there as soon as I can."

His arm dropped to his side like a leaden weight. Mrs.

Spigot pulled the phone from his hand and placed it in his back pocket before leading him out of the room and closing the door behind them.

Somehow, Jareth found himself back in the Rose Room, with no recollection as to how he had made his way there.

He lay on the bed feeling powerless and weak. The shivering had begun again, and no matter how his will pressed against it, his body would not be denied.

The last thought he had before passing into his healing sleep was a vow made to Florebelle:

You're the key to my heart, and I swear to do my damndest to bring you back to me. I love you now and forever, Flora.

Chapter Fourteen

Amira

Somebody better be dead.

That was the standard thing I uttered when someone dared to call after two in the morning. Let's face it, as I get older, that time is continually pushed back.

Now, I grumble when I get calls after 9:00 p.m. Especially if it's from work.

My hand shot out and slammed down in the general direction of where my phone should be on the nightstand.

After a few fumbling attempts, goodness only knew how many rings later, I answered.

Jareth? Why the hell would he be calling me at this hour?

"Hello?" My voice sounded like it belonged to a stranger because of the roughness from sleep with a layer of confusion and concern to top it off.

Silence.

"Jareth? Is that you? Is something wrong? Hello?"

"It's Flora. Can you come?"

Neither of us spoke until the silence was broken by a sob.

Adrenaline coursed through me, and I was wide awake in an instant.

My feelings shut down, and I ran through the logistics of getting to Orphic Cove. My brain ran like a supercomputer—there was no room for anxiety or any of the baser emotions.

"Yes, I'll be there as soon as I can."

Star was silhouetted in the doorway, a look of fear on her face.

"It's bad, isn't it?" she said to the darkness, not me.

It was reminiscent of the imaginary friend she talked to until college. The reminder of those dark times made me shudder.

"I didn't get any details, but Jareth was very"—I paused, trying to remember where my suitcase was—"emotional. I'm going to head out as soon as possible."

I couldn't up and leave right now. The earliest I could head out would be tonight. "Fuck."

Star swallowed. Her eyes were far away.

"I can go." She stepped back and leaned against the hallway wall as if in need of support. "I can fly out now. I'm certain Alexandre can pull a few strings and get me there straightaway."

"Does he have his own plane or something?"

She nodded partially to answer my question and partially to bolster her resolve. Even if I wanted to talk her out of it, it would be impossible now. When she had that look on her face, Star was unshakeable.

I wanted to stop her. Spending time with Alexandre wasn't the best thing for her mental health, but Star was a grown-assed woman, and our friend was obviously in need.

Plus, I sensed in my bones that this situation was bad. As in dire.

No, I might not exactly have been best friends with Jareth,

but that sob at the end of the call said it all. He was exhausted and terrified.

Alexandre was more than happy to wake up at this ungodly hour to help. He'd fly Star over himself.

With there being barely any street traffic and Star not needing much more than to change out of my old college shirt into her actual clothes, she grabbed her purse, and we headed out the door in under fifteen minutes.

As soon as we opened the exterior door to my building, a black limousine pulled up. I gave a furtive glance to Star, who shrugged.

"I didn't give him your address."

The chauffeur exited the car and opened the back door closest to the curb. He was wearing a black suit, white gloves, and shiny black shoes that looked like they were brand-new. No idea how the man was dressed and had arrived so fast.

Perhaps this Alexandre guy isn't so bad after all. Despite the weird effect he had on Star, his well-timed limo and access to private planes definitely makes him stand out in my book.

We piled into the vehicle and sped away to Alexandre's place.

Less than thirty minutes after the call from Jareth, Star and I stood on top of the fanciest building in Seattle. The rush of air from the whirling helicopter blades made me feel like I was trying to walk through a wind tunnel of epic force as I said my goodbyes to Star.

"I'll call you as soon as I get there." Star's hug lingered longer than I'd expected. When I saw Alexandre sitting in the pilot seat, his eyes were so trained on Star, it made me second-guess if the risk to Star was worth it. The heat and intensity of his stare was profoundly disturbing.

"Be safe, okay? I... I don't trust that Alexandre guy."

There. I'd said it. Now that I was fully in control of my faculties and not distracted by alcohol, I heard a thousand voices screaming: *"Stay away."*

And here I was, sending my friend right into the clutches of the dude that triggered the alert. If it weren't for Florebelle, I'd never have let her leave with him.

I gave one last wave as the screaming hunk of metal rose into the air. Star waved back.

Alexandre smirked.

Dammit. There's that ball of anxiety again.

Chapter Fifteen

Star

She craved him.

Amira had been right when she likened the way Star acted around Alexandre to being similar to an addict. She was disgusted with herself, feeling grateful for Jareth's call about Florebelle giving her an excuse to be with him.

Thibault told her Florebelle was fading fast and needed both of them in Orphic Cove as soon as possible. His appearing out of the blue like that to warn her had been startling. She hadn't seen him in years.

That wasn't altogether true.

She saw him often, lingering around the edges of things like a murky shadow, hovering *just* outside her peripheral vision, but she hadn't allowed him to talk to her at all for over six months. Thibault made everyone uncomfortable and wasn't known to be the bearer of good news.

Star pushed thoughts of Thibault's untimely return into the back of her mind as she readjusted herself in the narrow seat of the helicopter. Not really a fan of heights, she was grateful it was nighttime. There was no proper sense of depth to the city below on this cloudless night.

Hell, the twinkling lights are almost pretty.

"We'll be there before you know it."

His deeply resonant, commanding voice still affected her when it came over the headset.

Star squeezed her legs together and kept her eyes locked on the fast-moving terrain below.

She stayed quiet as a mouse.

Speaking to Alexandre now would only make him want to start up a conversation. *The less we talk, the less he can affect me. To be honest, it isn't like we're going to join the mile high club in a helicopter he's piloting, but if ever there was a time to be wrong about that, this isn't it.*

"Cat got your tongue?" He dropped his voice, making the bass undertones even deeper. If this kept up, Star didn't feel like she could control herself. She imagined them plunging toward the ground into a flaming pile of metal shards and glass.

Yes. That's a mood killer if ever there was one.

"I'm tired and worried. This is bad, Alexandre. I can feel it."

She allowed the negative emotions to wash over her. Not being used to them, Star was surprised to note how it was a cooling balm to the heat-filled horniness slowly coming to a fever pitch in her pants.

She would sigh in relief if she didn't feel like a completely out-of-control, hormone-driven monster.

"I understand. It must be serious to call me so late for something other than for me to shoot twixt wind and water."

What an odd turn of phrase. Sometimes he says things that make me wonder if he was even born in this century.

She knew this wasn't the first time she'd contemplated such things, but the errant thought faded away to obscurity.

Lost pockets of time were washed away in the carnal pleasure of their bodies becoming one.

Breath quickening, Star's hand fluttered to her forehead to wipe away a bead of sweat.

Shit. Think about Flora!

That did the trick.

For now.

Mind rising out of the gutter, Star thought it best to close her eyes and pretend to sleep.

How long before we get to the airport? Surely, a helicopter can't make it all the way to Maine?

When she woke up, they were in Orphic Cove.

More aptly, they were landing on the lawn in front of the bed-and-breakfast.

"How long was I asleep? And how did we make it all the way here in a helicopter?"

Alexandre turned off the chopper, removed her headset, and caressed her face lovingly. If she'd been squirrelier than her friends gave her credit for, she could swear the man was trying to mesmerize her.

So sleepy.

Confused and drowsy, Star blinked away her questions and suspicions, grateful they'd made it to Orphic Cove in what would appear to be record time, all thoughts of the trip making no sense entirely forgotten.

Alexandre exited and walked over to her side, holding out a hand to support Star on her way out so she wouldn't fall.

Always the gentleman.

Twirling her as if they were dance partners in a competition, he pulled her tight to his body and whispered into her ear. "I'm here if you need me." Emphasis on the word *need*.

She pulled away gently, even though every cell in her body wanted to rip his clothes off and do him on the lawn. Florebelle's needs surpassed her own. Amira was counting on her too.

Amira's probably waiting for my call. I have a job to do.

Thibault's smoky whisper of a body came into view. He was waving frantically, but she had to ignore him because she didn't want Alexandre, or anyone else in town, thinking she was batshit crazy.

They walked to the door. Mrs. Spigot opened it almost immediately before Star had a chance to even place her hand on the doorknob. The look of worry on her wrinkled face made Star squirm.

Despite the craziness the trio had dealt with the last time they were in this house—held prisoner by an evil fairy queen who'd sentenced them to death, combining their powers to bring Jareth back through some interdimensional portal— she'd never seen Mrs. Spigot look afraid.

The older woman casually made a warding gesture with her hand.

Interesting.

"I'm so happy you're here. It might be best if your friend stays at the bed-and-breakfast up the street. I'll call and tell them to expect you."

The black cat who frequented the porch most nights jumped up onto the banister and hissed, his back arched in a defensive posture. He was in pounce-and-attack mode. Wolves nestled in the thicket of woods across the street gave a bone-chilling howl. Everything went still.

"I'll be sure to check in later today to see how your friend's doing. Call me if you need me."

Alexandre was off like a flash, trotting down the porch steps, hurriedly making his way to whatever bed-and-breakfast Mrs. Spigot had referred him to.

Star yawned. It was nearly dawn, and she was grateful for the sleep she was able to get in the helicopter.

She felt sick to her stomach when she saw Florebelle tied to the bed. Her friend looked like a frail, broken version of herself. Jareth was nowhere in sight, and Mrs. Spigot looked like she was close to passing out.

"I'm so sorry, dear. Things here are quite the mess. I'm tempted to send for Mrs. Pettigrew again, but she said there's nothing she can do. Florebelle's been contaminated with some kind of darkness that's eating away at her soul." She tenderly pressed the damp washcloth to Florebelle's forehead. She reached out to brush back a curly tendril. Stopping short, she pulled her hand back and winced.

"She can't be touched." Mrs. Spigot sighed as if in pain.

"What can we do? There has to be *something* we can do." Star was frantic. Seeing one of her best friends like this was unbearable.

"There *is* one thing. Well, a person, really. She'll have the answers we seek."

"She?" Star wondered why she'd even asked, because she didn't care what the solution was. If there was a chance in hell to save Florebelle, she was going to agree to it.

No matter the price.

"Yes, but I need your help, love. And we'll have to do it soon." She placed a hand on Florebelle's shoulder, muttering under her breath, "There, that should buy us an hour or two. I'm tired after keeping her contained. Weaving that sleeping spell on you from such a distance also took a lot out of me."

"That was you?" The relief in Star's voice was palpable. She felt a pang of guilt remembering how she'd fallen asleep when her friend was in trouble.

"Yes. I didn't think you'd mind, considering the situation." Concern was etched into the lines around her eyes. She cracked a wan smile and continued, "Follow me, and we'll have a chat with an old friend." She stopped halfway to the door and turned, with a look of apprehension on her face. "You *can* speak to the dead, right?"

Star didn't know how to answer that. No one apart from the intake person at the psychiatric hospital she'd been evaluated at when she was eighteen had ever asked her that specifically.

It was something she'd had the common sense to keep to herself, even then.

"Not exactly." Thibault's shadowy head nodded gravely, signifying his willingness to help. "But...yes."

It was honorable of him after the way I treated him over the past couple of decades. Seemed like the only time I acknowledged his existence was when I needed something, and those times were few and far between. Until now.

She nodded back with a wry smile. A poor thank-you, but a thank-you nonetheless.

Mrs. Spigot gave her a curious, pensive look before making her way down the hallway. To goodness only knew where.

For a woman that short, she moved incredibly fast. So fast, in fact, Star was almost ashamed to say she had to jog to keep up with her.

Jareth

A set of scenes played through his mind in an endless loop.

The look of betrayal on Florebelle's face when she found out about his engagement to Hildesheim.

The knife flashing as she tried to stab him.

Mrs. Spigot using her magicks to lash her to the bed like a rabid dog.

He wasn't fully asleep. The healing rest that forced him into his own mind was a protective one, but not necessarily something where he wasn't in complete control of his faculties. Only having ever dealt with shadow walking between realms to the point of magickal exhaustion on one other occasion, he knew to count himself lucky, but the timing of this couldn't have been more atrocious.

Perhaps it would be best to think of other times.

Better times.

The moment Florebelle and I met on the train.

The squeal of the train wheels as they rounded the curve. And there she was. Careening wildly, completely out of control. She'd almost face-planted right in front of him.

The curvy goddess he'd seen bathed in light—like a beacon.

My fated mate.

He'd known since that moment. And all he did was stand there like a chump, mouth wide open, tongue on the floor, watching her run off to catch her train. Cursing himself because he'd lost his chance.

If I'd only known then what I know now.

He was happy with the progress of their journey together. Happy except for whatever darkness was consuming her.

That taint on her soul was taking the woman he loved farther and farther away from him.

And it hurt all the more because he knew it was at least partially his fault.

Someone, or something, else may have infected her with the darkness, but finding out about his engagement to Hildesheim was what had pushed her over the edge. She was worse off now, even after all Filene's ministrations.

Whatever happened from this moment forth would be a cross he'd have to bear for the rest of his natural life.

No amount of love is going to get us out of this mess.

It was time to rest, regain his equilibrium, and pray to the Goddess that Amira and Star could help.

Thankfully, he'd been able to make that one call before going into his healing sleep. Powerless as he was, he at least knew her sisters could take care of her in her time of need.

With self-recrimination came the barrage of scenes again, in full color, fresh as when they'd first transpired.

The look of betrayal on Florebelle's face when she found out about his engagement to Hildesheim.

The knife flashing as she tried to stab him.

Mrs. Spigot using her magicks to lash her to the bed like a rabid dog...

Chapter Sixteen

Star

"I don't need all this," Star said in awe.

Mrs. Spigot had brought her to a new room that was like the one she and her friends had been in when they'd saved Jareth from the fae queen's evil clutches. Every square inch of the place was so full of tallow candles, the local fire department would give them a citation and a stern warning if they ever found out.

"This room was built specifically for those who channel. There are wards engraved into the walls, floor, and ceiling to ensure no evil spirits can pass through. It's a safe space where your talents will be magnified significantly."

Star kept quiet. Mrs. Spigot often spoke to her as if she had the vaguest idea of what the older woman was talking about. Most of the time she'd spent with her since coming to the Witch's House involved a lot of nodding and keeping her mouth shut so she didn't look like a fool.

"You'll want to reach out to Sarah Good." Mrs. Spigot handed Star a silver ring. "Here."

She turned the ring over in her hand, inspecting it. It was a simple thing, well-worn and weathered, an antique. Star slipped the ring onto her finger, eager to get started, but nervous about what lay ahead.

I can't fail Flora, and Amira put her trust in me to hold down the fort until she gets here.

With a clenched jaw, Star scanned the room.

There!

Hiding in a suspiciously dust-free corner was the perfect chair. It was overstuffed and looked cushy as all get-out. Star plopped into it, wriggling around for a few seconds until she was comfortable.

It's time to get my meditation on.

Legs up in a lotus position, hands resting on her knees, she closed her eyes, sat up straight, and breathed with intention.

Inhale, two, three, four. Hold, two, three, four. Exhale, two, three, four.

All the worry, fear, and wayward thoughts of Alexandre and Florebelle melted away as she sank into the core of her being. When she finally reached a state of relaxation and calm, she opened her eyes and called out to Thibault.

"Guide me, friend. Lead me to Sarah Good."

There was no pomp or ceremony necessary.

Thibault, silent as always, darted past what appeared to be a foggy veil that hovered between her and the rest of the room. This part always seemed to go in slow motion. It was difficult to be patient. To just relax into the present, release all expectations, and accept that she was nothing more than a conduit.

Her job was to breathe and keep any invasive thoughts from derailing her. Maintaining steadfast concentration was the most important task. It was what kept the path between the living world and the dead open. She was the bridge between the two.

Inhale, two, three, four. Hold, two, three, four. Exhale, two, three, four.

Intense fear crept around the edges, trying to bleed through. Star didn't recall it ever taking quite this long for Thibault to bring a soul back through the veil.

No matter, I just have to wait. I just have to...

Inhale, two, three, four. Hold, two, three, four. Exhale, two, three, four.

Star continued the pattern until she felt a slender thread.

"Sarah?" she asked into the dark reddish haze of her closed eyelids.

"It is I," Sarah said, voice light as a feather.

When Star opened her eyes, she saw the spectral woman before her, dressed in dark, drab clothes that faded in and out of the mist of the veil. The first few inches of her brunette hair were parted down the center. The rest lay hidden under a bonnet.

"Hello, Sarah," Star said as she waved Mrs. Spigot close and reached out her hand. The older woman stood beside her and placed her hand on Star's.

Once the connection was made between them, Mrs. Spigot gasped.

"Sarah, oh my Sarah!"

"You can see her?" Star asked incredulously. This was a first. Not that anyone had ever touched her while she was channeling and talking to spirits before.

She saw Thibault grinning knowingly to himself in a dark corner of the room ten feet away.

"Why hast thou brought me across the veil, Goody Spile? It must be a reason of great import?"

"Aye, it is indeed, my most beloved friend. There's a darkness eating away at a young witch. We do not know from whence it came, but it reminds me of the story you told of Mistress Rowan."

"A blight most terrible, it was. Mistress Rowan required the aid of our entire coven to remove the stain upon her soul. We three waged battle with that taint for nearly half a day. Almost perished, we did, from the strain and suffering of it all. In the end, we persevered with the aid of the Book of Sins. What an ironical name." She chuckled to herself. The laughter grew weak toward the end.

"I miss you," Mrs. Spigot said in a whisper with a catch in her throat.

"I miss thee as well, Goody Spile. There be naught to fear when passing through the veil. I'll spend an eternity with the sisters who came before us. We feel no more pain over the sufferings endured in our long, harrowed lives." Her wan smile brightened against her dimming figure.

"She has to go now," Star said to Mrs. Spigot. "She's fading, and I can't keep the connection open much longer."

Sarah was drawn back toward the veil, floating across the floor with a fluttering of petticoats roiling like puffs of smoke blown from an old man's pipe. The scent of ozone grew strong.

It was time.

Star sent a mental call out to Thibault, but he was nowhere to be found. She needed him to lead the spirit of Sarah Good back through the veil.

The tether keeping her here was weakening, as was Star. Several decades had passed since she'd last done a calling, and like atrophied muscles, she'd grown weak from the lack of use. Despite the sigils in the room bolstering her powers, she was fading fast.

It was hard to breathe, and the world was wobbly.

Where are you, Thibault? Goddess knows I don't want to find out what happens to spirits who don't make it back in time, and I surely don't want to be responsible for the aftermath.

"Fare thee well, sister. Until we meet again." Sarah's voice was barely a whisper. She was drawn back, yet closer to the veil.

"Goodbye, sister," Mrs. Spigot replied. Star felt the reluctance as her friend removed her hand to wipe away the tears sliding down her cheeks.

The moment the two disconnected, Thibault reappeared with a sheepish look on his face. With one gray, shadowed hand outstretched, Sarah Good grabbed on and followed him through the veil back to the world of the dead.

When both passed through to the other side, Sarah's glow brightened. She stopped, turned, and spoke, her voice somehow stronger than it was before.

"Beware the dark one who wishes to stand by thy side. The feelings he invokes are not natural. Listen to thy will, thy heart, and thy sisters."

With that, she disappeared, not in a flash of light, but like the last tendril of morning fog broken up by a gust of wind.

Star was stunned.

No one had ever talked to her from the other side of the veil before.

Inhale, two, three, four. Hold, two, three, four. Exhale, two, three, four.

Amira

I was pissed.

Susan never showed up. Didn't even call to cancel her appointment.

Right before shutting down my laptop and heading off to court, I received an email from her.

"False alarm. Mr. Goatnuts had Melanie dropped off at my apartment this morning with papers transferring custody back to me. We won! It's a miracle."

What the hell?

I read her email three times, the words not quite registering because of the nonsensical nature of the whole thing. Glancing at the clock, I realized I had just enough time to leave a voicemail and hope she called back with more details on whatever the heck had happened.

It was highly unlikely what she said was kosher. I mean, why would her gloating ex-husband just drop Melanie off with her mother? And how did he get papers transferring custody that quickly?

I grabbed my jacket and stuffed my briefcase with the last few papers necessary for my next hearing before heading out the door. Hopefully, my ride would get here soon. This day needed to end so I could get to Maine.

My heart wasn't in it. I just wanted to be with Florebelle. Never the most intuitive of our trio, I still knew something big was brewing and that my presence was required, not optional.

Stupid adulting. Stupid partnership. I'd probably call in sick if it weren't for them dangling that carrot in front of me.

"Hey, Susan. This is Amira Rapaport from Bankton, Rockman, Hughes, and Wins. Just wanted to get some clarification on your email. Are you saying your ex-husband returned Melanie to you with paperwork showing transfer of custody?"

I waved at the car heading toward me, which matched the rideshare app description. "Call me back so I can make sure everything's in order. Talk to you soon."

This afternoon was going to be a colossal pain in the ass. I wanted to head straight to the airport after work and catch a flight.

Why the hell hasn't Star called me yet? Is she in trouble too?

Once the car door closed and the seat belt lock clicked, the emotional part of my brain turned off and I went into work mode.

That click made all the distractions of mood and personal problems fade away. I focused on the case at hand. Your standard divorce fare. The husband violated the prenup and would have to give his soon-to-be ex-wife her fair share. He didn't even attempt to fight it. That meant one of two things. Either he was still hoping beyond hope that by not being an argumentative cuss, he'd win her back in the end, or what she didn't know about was far, far worse than what he'd done and he was afraid of the truth getting out.

As far as the getting-back-together scenario was concerned—fat chance. In my experience, when the wife was the one to end it, they rarely gave their exes a second chance.

Star

"How did she get free?" Jareth asked. The calmness he displayed spoke volumes. He was exhausted, worn ragged, concerned, but still somehow managed to keep it all together.

After waking from his healing sleep, much too soon to be fully recovered, he found Florebelle putting nightshade berries into Star's cup of tea. Mrs. Spigot had left it steeping by Star's bed. It was by the luck of the Goddess he just happened to pass by the door when he did.

Florebelle hadn't even tried to hide her activities.

"I just lay down for a minute," Mrs. Spigot sputtered. Having never seen her nonplussed before, no one seemed to know what to do. Mrs. Spigot wove another spell on the sleeping Florebelle. "She'll be out for several hours now. We're going to have to hurry, Star. I know you're exhausted."

"But we need Amira," she pleaded, still shocked by the fact one of her best friends had tried to poison her.

How did she even know how to use the nightshade? Her only experience with flora and fauna was the occasional visit to botanical gardens and zoos.

She shuddered as her brain tried to process what had just happened.

Jareth was so weak, he could barely help Mrs. Spigot lift the slumbering Florebelle and return her to his room.

He tripped. The sudden imbalance almost took down Mrs. Spigot as she buckled under the full weight of Florebelle's limp body. Star grabbed her friend and held her up as she took Jareth's place.

"It's going to be okay. Trust me. You need to rest."

He looked defeated. Nodding, he scratched his pallid cheek before making his way down the hallway in abject silence.

Shit... I never called Amira!

Reaching for her phone, Star cursed herself for her forgetful ways.

Of all the times to be flighty, this wasn't one of them. Amira's probably a nervous wreck by now!

Wide-awake after the rush of adrenaline of both the murder attempt and the shame of forgetting her promise to Amira, she dialed her friend, counting each ring until it went to voicemail.

"Amira. We need you."

Chapter Seventeen

Amira

The voicemail from Star shook me to the core.

Star must have been scared shitless, because she sounded like a child. My normally loquacious friend was reduced to four words. She'd never, to my recollection, left a voicemail that short.

As soon as court was over, I made a beeline to the airport with nothing more than my purse, briefcase, and the clothes on my back. They put me on a flight leaving thirty minutes after I arrived. The Goddess was with me, because I made it to the gate just in time to board before they closed the plane's doors.

I couldn't eat or drink or think.

Every ounce of my being was focused on getting to Portland, Maine. To be there for my friend. My imagination was racing.

Star—the queen of TMI—hadn't given me any details. That was so unlike her.

By the time my flight landed, I had to have listened to the

voicemail about fifty times. I tried to decipher what I could from the nuance of each vague word from Star's voicemail.

"Amira. We need you." That was it. That was all I had to work with.

I flagged down a taxi about fifteen minutes after the plane landed. One perk of traveling without luggage was the nearly nonexistent wait time.

I'd snagged a first-class ticket, and telling the flight attendant I had an emergency that necessitated getting off first actually worked.

I was just lucky I didn't mow someone down on my way to the taxi stand at the pace I was running—in heels.

"Orphic Cove, please."

"Say what?" the driver asked incredulously. "That's pretty far away, lady. I'm not sure I—"

"I'll pay you an extra five hundred dollars if you get me there in the next hour. And don't call me 'lady.'"

His eyes lit up when I pulled a wad of money out of my purse. Before I had time to put my seat belt on, he swerved into traffic, slamming his foot down on the gas.

Not safe, but the rapid acceleration soothed my burgeoning anxiety. I'd get to my friends soon or die trying.

Jareth

"Max. Can you meet up at Clancy's? I know it's pretty last minute."

"Sure, man. I'll be there in five."

That was one thing he liked about Max. As much shit as they gave each other, he was always there for Jareth in a pinch. It went both ways. They'd gotten each other out of more jams throughout their lives than two law-abiding citizens ever should.

Five minutes later, Max strode in, sliding into the booth across from him. He reached for the menu and read it. So pointless. He always ordered the same thing at Clancy's without fail.

"Your usual?" the waitress asked him. She seemed to come out of nowhere, undoubtedly attracted to him. Most women acted like that when Max came around. It was like the guy was steeped in pheromones.

He smiled and nodded. "Thanks, Doreen. You're a gem."

She beamed back at him. Her craggy face lit up like the sun. Her smile was truly magnetic and, under normal circumstances, likely quite infectious.

For obvious reasons, Jareth wasn't in the mood to smile.

"How about you, sonny?" She looked at Jareth expectantly with her pen hovering over her pad.

She'd served him hundreds of times, but every time was like the first time. He didn't even register on her radar. The only woman who looked at him the way they did at Max was Flora.

"A water's good for now." She was annoyed. Jareth was reminded by her furrowed brow that her pay was based on what her customers ordered. He often forgot about such silly customs. "Can you just get me what he's having? And a coffee. Thanks."

Doreen went from annoyed to jovial. Her lips curled up at the edges as she looked him up and down. "You sure, hon? That's a whole heap of food."

Jareth nodded without bothering to respond. It wasn't as if he were planning on actually eating anything. He was too sick to bother.

With menus and orders taken, it was time to get down to

145

business.

"Something's wrong with Flora. I don't know how to handle this, Max."

"Must be serious, mate. You haven't called me Maxi-pad once during our last two conversations. That's got to be a first." His laughing eyes grew somber. "What's going on?"

"She tried to kill me and one of her best friends. It's some kind of sickness. It's so advanced, even Filene can't handle it." Max's eyebrows knit together in concern. Jareth knew he was holding something back. "What's on your mind, brother? Spit it out."

Max did a quick scan of the diner to ensure no one was within hearing range. He leaned in, the intensity of his gaze deepening. "I smelled something, man. The scent reminded me of Queen Diaphne. It was dark and evil. Rotten. I sensed the same thing when I went for a run in the woods near the Witch's House a couple of weeks back."

At a loss for words, Jareth waited in silence. Waiting for the empty air to fill with the cursed words he feared his friend would speak aloud.

"I think she's infected with whatever drove Diaphne mad."

They'd suspected it for decades.

The stories of her benevolence and wisdom seemed but a fairy tale because the queen they'd grown to hate over the past century was nothing like the stories they'd been fed in child-hood. Rumors had spread through cautious whispers about her being cursed.

Now, not only might those rumors be true, but she might have passed this curse on to Flora.

Jareth believed Max implicitly. Especially when it came to his nose.

"One more thing. There's a vampire in town. Came in a

few hours ago."

"You've got to be kidding me."

Doreen with the infectious smile returned with several plates piled high with nearly raw meat.

She placed three plates in front of him. Another waitress with short red hair and green eyes trailed behind her, carrying three more, which she placed in front of Max.

She lingered longer than was necessary, no doubt because of his pheromones.

Hildesheim had once told him Max smelled welcoming, woodsy, and wild.

It was all Jareth could do not to gag at the sight of all the blood. Max chuckled to himself because he knew what his friend's reaction would be well before the food came.

Instant payback for all the times I called him a female hygiene product.

Jareth pushed his plates across the table closer to Max as he cracked his knuckles and tore into the flesh of at least half a cow.

"Mmm, mmm, good. Gotta love the Friday night special." His words were barely comprehensible as his mouth was muffled by massive quantities of bloody meat.

"Remind me to never come here with you on a Friday again."

"Your loss," he said as he stabbed at the steak on Jareth's plate and dragged it onto his own.

Star

"Amira sent a text. She's taking a cab from the airport. Should be here within the hour." She almost sighed in relief. Just knowing Amira was finally in the same state was reassurance enough, but that she was less than an hour away? *We might be able to do this after all.* "Is there anything I can do?"

Mrs. Spigot grimaced as she shook her head. The beads of sweat on her forehead stood out in stark relief against her furrowed brow. The droplets were on the verge of streaming down her face in rivulets.

Star felt powerless. The older woman was tiring rapidly. Keeping Florebelle asleep was draining her fast, and there was nothing she could do to help.

The poor woman won't be able to keep this up for long.

Star wrung her hands like a nervous old biddy.

Scared, helpless, and not knowing what to do? These weren't feelings she was used to. Being in control of herself was the norm. Everything started crumbling once she'd gotten reacquainted with Alexandre.

It was hard to believe they'd seen each other for the first time in months just a couple of days ago.

That was by her choice.

Alexandre had been reluctant to let her go, but she'd had to do it for her own sanity.

It was difficult not to blame at least some of the craziness on him. Apart from what happened the last time she, Amira, and Florebelle were in Orphic Cove, she hadn't had this much disaster in her life since her adolescence.

Right before college, to be precise. The time they put her in a mental hospital.

She couldn't help herself. The recollection of the psychiatric hospital made her subconsciously scan the room for Thibault. He'd been the harbinger of doom back in the day. One of the many reasons she fought so hard to pretend he didn't exist for the last few decades of her life.

Having him as a constant companion was enough to drive

anyone mad, but today, she had to admit he'd come through in a pinch.

Picking up a fresh washcloth from the pile beside Florebelle's bed, she went over to Mrs. Spigot and mopped her brow. She gave Star a small, tight smile. The weariness in her eyes was unsettling.

It was clear she was holding on through sheer grit and determination.

"My God. How strong is Flora?" As soon as the question left her mouth, she realized Mrs. Spigot wouldn't answer. Couldn't answer. In fact, she grunted as she pushed her hands straight out in front of her chest in a protective fashion.

It looked like she was attempting to push away an angry, charging rhino.

Her arms quivered with tension, and her jaw was clenched so hard, Star was surprised she didn't hear Mrs. Spigot's teeth shattering to dust.

Amira

The cab driver more than earned his five hundred dollars. He got me to the driveway of the Witch's House within thirty minutes. I was fairly certain if there had been any cops on the road, the man would have gotten his driver's license revoked and lost his job.

I felt bad about the hypothetical situation and tossed him another couple of hundred before collecting my meager belongings and bolting for the front door.

Most expensive cab ride of my life, but it was worth it. I walked right into the house. This was the first time I'd come into the house with no gleeful, smiling Mrs. Spigot to greet me.

The grandiose building didn't have the same ambiance as it normally did. When we first came here to surprise Florebelle on her birthday, the place was full of warmth and fall scents, rife with the aromas of cinnamon, apple cider, and ginger.

It made you want to curl up in a ball on one of the comfy couches in the main area with a cup of tea and a blanket.

Today, despite the merry Christmas decorations, presents, and an endless sea of red ribbon bows scattered everywhere, it felt cold and sterile. Soulless. Empty.

I didn't know which room they were in. The bed-and-breakfast was huge. It might take ages to find them. I pulled out my phone to text Star and was startled when she popped out from behind a corner.

"Thank the Goddess. I wasn't expecting you for another half hour. Come on, we have to hurry. Mrs. Spigot can't handle her for much longer."

I raced after my friend down the hallway, up two sets of stairs, and down another passage. When we finally arrived in the room, I stopped dead.

Florebelle was tied to the bed with rope, and Mrs. Spigot looked like she'd been kicked by a mule.

Maybe kicked more than once.

"Tell us what to do." It was time to get down to business. We had to get started on doing something for Mrs. Spigot and Florebelle. Without the former's guidance, we had no chance in hell of helping the latter.

"The Book of Sins. It's in my pocket." She gasped, gritting her teeth against some invisible force that caused her great pain. "Open it, and it will tell you the spell. Star can't touch it. She mustn't touch it." Mrs. Spigot went flying backward, her

150

arms still out, ramrod straight, as her back thunked against the wall.

Under normal circumstances, I would have been full of questions, suspicion, and a more than healthy dose of skepticism.

But these were *not* normal circumstances.

I reached into her pocket and opened the small book I fished out without so much as glancing at the cover.

The words on the page were blurry, moving around like sea foam on the surface of a wave.

Shit. I can't read this!

With fears mounting, it was as if the entire universe stopped. I stilled, and my mind went into work mode. All emotions were placed on the back burner until the task was complete. I beckoned Star over with a jerk of my head. She came close to touching the book, but I tugged it back before her fingers came in contact with it.

"You can't touch it. I don't know why, but you mustn't touch it." She shook her head. I could tell she very much wanted to handle the book. She looked almost like she did when Alexandre was near. That same sense of craving.

"I can't read it," Star said dreamily as she reached out, almost connecting with it once again.

Mrs. Spigot moaned. With great effort, she spat out a few words. "Hold hands."

I transferred the book to my left hand and grabbed Star's with my right.

"I can make out the words now," Star confirmed.

"We'll read on the count of three," my friend said. I bobbed my head in agreement. "One. Two. Three."

We read the words from the page in unison.

Chapter Eighteen

Jareth

After a short walk back from Clancy's, the two men entered the Witch's House. The preternatural silence was punctuated by a scream that sounded like Mrs. Spigot.

Shit, am I too late?

Jareth was about to duck into the nearest shadow so he could travel to the room in an instant, but realized at the last moment Max would have to find his way on his own.

Dammit.

He ran to the room as fast as he could. Max easily overtook him with long, fluid strides.

Max turned his head to the side and spoke with the steady cadence of a man standing still. "Take to the shadows." He then doubled his speed and was gone in a flash.

Jareth ducked into the first patch of black he could find, reappearing a few seconds later in the corner of Florebelle's room.

Mrs. Spigot lay on the floor moaning, arms stretched out,

warding off something that was rapidly draining her significant magickal resources.

Star and Amira read aloud from a small red book covered in gold writing. It pulsed in the light like a beating heart. With each word they spoke, a dark whisper of a shadow deepened around Florebelle.

The thin, dark strand reached out toward Jareth. As it grew closer, it darted out like a striking viper.

He took a step back at the last moment, dipping into the shadow he'd just stepped out of, came out from behind the open door, then scuttled into the safety of the hallway. Just in time to crash into Max.

"They're doing some kind of spell," he said under his breath to his newly arrived friend. He didn't budge from the doorway to ensure neither of them got caught up by the ever-growing noxious black cloud.

With his gaze firmly on Star, Max wrinkled his nose and growled, low and deep.

"That vampire's stench is all over her."

Jareth had never seen Max like this. Another concern for another day. This wasn't the time or the place for questions. He could only worry or wonder about one person.

Florebelle.

Both men's eyes swept back and forth between the women who continued reading, Mrs. Spigot's supine body, and Florebelle—who was writhing in the bed as if she were possessed by a demon.

Whatever language the women were speaking was unknown to him, but he knew it wasn't of human origin. He realized they were repeating the same words again and again.

He and Max stood outside the doorway, ready to leap to action at a moment's notice if the women needed their help.

Knowing these two, we're wasting our time. These women are no helpless damsels in distress.

The sinister cloud grew denser and more ominous, inching closer and closer to Star and Amira, slow as molasses.

The women continued repeating the words until their throats grew raw.

Mrs. Spigot was now passed out at their feet with her back against the wall. She wore a tranquil expression at odds with what was going on around her.

I hope her dreams are more pleasant than our reality.

Star

The words they spoke weren't any language she'd ever heard before, which was surprising. Not only because she'd traveled to almost every country on this planet to learn green witch-craft, or because she was disturbingly good at picking up languages. It was because, despite not knowing the language, she could still understand what they were saying.

The words, as written, were complete gobbledygook, mostly because they were phonetic, but once she connected with Amira and spoke them aloud, her brain translated them into English.

Here lies the damned
   Tarnished by the darkest curse
   Let us scrub the victim clean of her sins
   And steal the darkness into ourselves
   So that we may feast upon it

                    .   .   .

The words were creepy as hell, but also comforting.

The comfort she took as she said each verse was what she found most disturbing. As they spoke in what felt like a never-ending loop, their eyes never leaving the book even though they'd memorized each word long ago, Star felt an indescribable presence encroaching upon them, and she delighted in it.

She felt an exhilaration that was almost sublime, like being on the verge of a most carnal pleasure. It made all the hairs on her body stand up at attention and made her tingle in the most delicious places.

Truth be told, she wished the darkness would come over them faster. She wanted to dip her toes in it. Swim in it. She wanted to absorb it into herself and knew she would treasure it always.

She craved the darkness.

And she coveted the book.

Star wanted both more than she'd ever wanted anything ever before in her entire life. That desire kept her focused. Her only chance of obtaining both was to see this through to the end.

Her throat burned, but still they chanted, long into the night. The dark smoke curled closer to the women standing hand in hand, caught between the passed-out form of Mrs. Spigot and the two men anxiously observing from the hallway.

At the point where they were unsure if they could say another single word, the shadow reached out and touched them.

Star shuddered with delight. Amira tried to let go of her hand, but they were linked to each other like conjoined twins.

Amira

I tried to scream, but my voice was gone.

All I could do was ride the waves along with Star as the darkness filled us up like no man ever had before.

We woke up on the floor. Jareth stood over me, eyes full of concern as he scanned to find any visible damage.

"I'm okay. Check on Flora." My voice was that of a stranger, coming from a throat cut by a thousand shards of glass. The way it felt, I was surprised I wasn't drowning in my own blood.

He nodded, giving one last scrutinizing glance before stepping over me and making his way to the bed.

I wasn't able to see her face from my position, but I could tell from his body language that whatever we had done had worked.

To my left, I saw a lumbering figure standing over Star. It was Jareth's friend, Max. I knew Jareth had come into the room, but I'd been so absorbed in the spell, I wasn't aware he'd brought someone with him.

Mrs. Spigot sat in a chair near the window. Though pale, her face was cheery as always. Her usually radiant smile was thin. A carefully constructed façade meant to lessen our worry. If you looked past it, it wasn't hard to see the barely covered grimace of pain.

A door closed somewhere down the hallway, immediately followed by the rhythmic click of high heels, which grew louder as they rapidly approached us.

A gray-haired older woman with a nose like a bird's beak strode in. She was calm, cool, collected, and ominous as fuck.

I felt like a cockroach being brought into the light. I wanted to scurry and hide as soon as she came fully into view.

The newcomer didn't even glance at Star, me, or the men. She only had eyes for Florebelle.

"I guess you succeeded?" We knew her question was directed to Mrs. Spigot despite her laser focus on my bedbound friend.

Mrs. Spigot shrugged and slumped in the chair. The crone went to the bed and placed her hands on either side of Florebelle's head.

I was frozen in fear.

The courageous part of me wanted to jump up and knock her hands off my friend, but my body wouldn't have anything to do with such lofty ideas. I lay there on the floor, near paralyzed from exhaustion, unable to speak through my seared throat.

"She's not fully healed, but how did you..." Her voice trailed off as she walked over to Star. Max didn't budge an inch as she bent over. I swear I heard him growl like a feral cat, but figured it was just my mind playing tricks on me.

She placed her hands on either side of Star's head and closed her eyes. Her head sharply bobbed one time—with so much force I thought her long, pointy chin would surely poke through the parchment-thin flesh of her upper chest.

"Seems like your guests saved the day." She lowered her head one more time and uttered something under her breath. "You all have about two months before the L'i'al Dool takes you over. I'd be most concerned about this one." She pointed at Florebelle. "Keep an eye on her. Not as if there's much you can do."

She twitched her head in Florebelle's direction and stood, smoothing her jet-black skirt against her thighs.

"Who are you?" I whispered.

"Save your voice, dear. You're going to need it later." She gave me a withering look on the tail end of a derisive sneer.

That single glance made me feel smaller and weaker than I did before. A powerful heat flooded my body, making my fingertips itch.

She was off like a shot, heading down the hallway the same way she'd come, never looking behind or slowing her pace. The only sign of her presence was the steady click of her heels as she made her way down the hallway.

Star

When she woke up, she felt different. Not in a way she could precisely put a finger on, but she somehow inherently knew something had been altered. In that "forever changed" kind of way.

For better or worse, I've sealed my fate.

Ever since she was a child, Star could see other people's futures in the cards. Everyone's but her own and those she considered family.

It was always a great mystery, except for two things. She knew when she hit her forties, she'd burst forth into the world a new being—metamorphosed like a caterpillar turning into a butterfly. The other fact was something she wished she could scrub from her memory, because it was far from positive.

She knew how she was going to die.

Star tried not to dwell on the whole death thing very much. There was no actual point in it. After all, she had decades, oodles of decades, to live for. She was old and gray and shriveled in the vision. She'd barely aged since hitting twenty-two.

But today, today was the day she burst forth from her cocoon.

She couldn't quite tell if the path she was on was a good one or not, but she felt powerful. As an adult, she'd always felt powerful in herself, but this was different.

Well, until the day I met Alexandre.

The power he had over her was daunting.

Turnabout's fair play. If this is how the men who crave me feel on the daily, they have my heartfelt sympathy.

Star smiled wryly at the trail of broken hearts she'd left behind over the past thirty years, starting when she'd hit puberty.

Boys were after her like she was a dog in heat.

And they did pretty much whatever she wanted whenever she wanted. It wasn't until she was in her midtwenties that she'd realized she had a choice to either use and abuse people for her own whims or to be a powerful force of good in the world.

She'd opted to give the latter the good ole college try. That was how she fell into being a green witch.

But this L'i'al Dool? She could feel it changing her somehow. The intense animalistic pleasure she felt when it overtook her woke something deep within the core of her being. Like a sleeping dragon brought out into the light—it was hungry.

It was ravenous.

And it would not be denied.

Star opened her eyes and saw Max straddling her.

Surprise, surprise. Perhaps this is my lucky day, after all?

There was something about the man she found most compelling. He wasn't as enthralled with her as most of the guys who followed her around like lost puppy dogs.

And the way he smells? Absolutely yummy. Musky, with a hint of deep, dark, rich forest loam.

A scent she was particularly attracted to because of

160

spending a significant amount of time searching for herbs, plants, and such for her tinctures, teas, and potions in lush forests throughout the world.

"It's about time you woke up." His voice was a concerned growl that made her grin from ear to ear like the Cheshire cat.

He grunted and stepped off her, excitement pronounced. She caught a glimpse before he untucked his shirt and turned away, face darkening in embarrassment.

Chapter Nineteen

Jareth

Everyone but Max and Mrs. Spigot slept in the room with Florebelle. The two girls lay in the bed with her while Jareth camped out in the overstuffed chair in the corner. His feet rested on a small chest he'd dragged in from a room down the hall.

They all took turns watching over her.

Mrs. Spigot needed time to recover. The experience had drained her normally hale and hearty self. She now looked older and more worn out than when she'd initially collapsed after being drained dry of her magicks.

Her smile was forced, and her skin was as thin and fragile as the paper from her centuries-old tomes.

Star and Amira stopped by her room a few times to check on her, but she always waved them off, telling them to go look after Florebelle.

Jareth barely budged from his spot. There was the occasional use of the bathroom. Fortunately, food magickally appeared outside the door every few hours. Snacks, drinks, and meals no one had the stomach to eat.

All physical urges or thoughts of anything besides if, or when, Florebelle would ever wake up were pushed aside.

After three days, she finally showed signs of life.

Her fluttering eyelids breathed new hope into each of them.

Perhaps the long wait will finally be over? Perhaps we can go back to life being the way it was?

Star and Max seemed to have become fast friends despite the situation and lack of talking. He'd occasionally pop into the room to *check on us,* but his gaze and attentions mostly seemed focused on her.

There. Did she just open her eyes?

Jareth jumped up from his seat and practically flew over to the bed.

"Florebelle?" He placed a hand on her cheek. Both of the friends had left a few minutes ago. If Florebelle were truly awake, perhaps he could have a few precious moments alone to find out if she was back to her normal self. "Flora. I'm here. It's Jareth. You have to wake up soon. Star, Amira, and I— everyone's really worried about you."

Guilt. Did I really go there? Yes. And I'd do it again.

"Mmmm." Her moan made his heart skip a beat. She was one step closer to waking up. It took everything within him not to shake her in his haste to get her to fully open her eyes and rise from the bed.

Patience. You must be patient.

"Jareth?"

He did something he hadn't done in at least a century—he cried like a baby.

Amira

We knew the instant Star and I returned to the room—Florebelle was awake. After three harrowing days, she was finally awake!

We rushed to her bedside like a stampede of cattle, hardly giving her any breathing room. It couldn't be helped. We all felt entitled to a few seconds of assurance before we left her to rest.

It was time to rejoice, and rejoice we did.

"Girl, I swear, if you had died, I would have killed you." Bad joke, I know, but I couldn't help myself. Sometimes I made bad jokes when I was nervous or anxious. Sue me.

Star puttered around the bed, fluffing things after setting down a steaming mug of some herbal concoction meant to reinvigorate and promote faster healing. After doing her rounds on the pillows, she swooped up the mug, blew on it a few times, and gently placed it into Florebelle's hands.

Florebelle grabbed the mug like it was a lifeline, warming her fingers and savoring the sensation for a moment before lifting it to her nose. "This smells like swamp water and a boatload of boiled egg farts. Are you trying to kill me?"

Florebelle was back, with her quick wit and occasional snark. Her hands and voice might be shaky, but her mind was intact.

I could feel waves of relief coming off Jareth, who stood behind me. He had red eyes and damp cheeks when we came rushing in. Whatever reservations I might have had about with him were eradicated. He loved her to pieces. That much I could tell.

She deserved as much. Maybe one day, I'd deserve love too.

I shook my head, annoyed at the narcissistic thought. This

wasn't a time for self-reflection or self-pity. This was a time to be elated that our friend was back in the world of the living.

"So, how do we celebrate Florebelle's return?" Mrs. Spigot's voice startled us.

I grasped her hand in mine, pumping it vigorously. "Thank you. A thousand times." I brought her in close for a hug. "Thank you."

She seemed surprised.

As did Florebelle and Star, judging from their expressions. Not being much of a hugger or a thanker, this was a bit out of character for me, but the appreciation I had for this woman couldn't be expressed enough.

The day I visited her during her recovery? Well, let's just say she looked like she wouldn't make it to morning. I had been half tempted to tell Star to stay away because I didn't want that to be the last memory she had of the dear old woman. I wasn't sure, but it seemed like they had gotten fairly close in their short time together.

Not like that wasn't par for the course with Star.

I felt Star's arms wrap around Mrs. Spigot. With the creak of the mattress, another shakier set as Florebelle joined in.

We stood that way, holding each other—locked in a loving embrace of friendship and sisterhood. Before long, Jareth moved in, coming up behind Florebelle.

"What have we got here? Should I get in on this?" Max's voice was jocular, yet affectionate, tinged with a hint of relief. Surprising, since he barely knew any of us besides Jareth.

"I think it's time I told you about the L'i'al Dool and the Book of Sins."

Mrs. Spigot's muffled voice rose through the layers of fabric, human bodies, and love. Being the shortest of us all, she looked like a child being surrounded by overly affectionate adults.

I was surprised she hadn't been crushed.

"Yes. We should definitely know what shitstorm we're up against."

Star

Florebelle was recovering faster than we could ever have hoped. She navigated the stairs with Jareth watching over her like a mother hen.

Everyone settled in the main room downstairs. It was packed full of comfy chairs and Christmas ornaments. Each of us was cradling a mug of some hot beverage on our laps when Mrs. Spigot cleared her throat and began speaking.

"Back in the Eldritch Times, as we witches used to call it, there was a creature known only as The Abomination." She waved her hands in the air, and the room filled with mist. When it cleared, we were all sitting in our seats, mugs in hand, but the room had changed to a forest scene with ghostly trees swaying in an imaginary breeze.

"Whoa, what the hell?" Amira squeaked as she jumped, nearly spilling her tea in her lap.

Star raised a finger to her lips, eyebrow raised, begging her to shush. Creating something as immersive as this took great power. And she, for one, really wanted to enjoy the moment. It was a rare treat to be brought into someone else's memories. She'd only experienced it once before, and accidentally done it herself during her time at the mental hospital when she was drugged beyond belief.

It hadn't ended well.

Mrs. Spigot cleared her throat and continued, "The Abomination was a taint upon the world. No one knew where it came from, but we realized it must be defeated, because its stain began covering large parts of the earth in darkness. The Abomination was an evil so intense, it warped the minds of man and fae. Anyone exposed was infected."

Dark tendrils of fog swept forth across the land with increasing speed. It reminded Star of a massive version of what they'd seen in the room when they'd chanted the spell to Florebelle. The animals it touched mutated before their very eyes. Men and fae creatures, once frolicking together, became violent.

The world was laid out before them like an unfolded map. Blood pooled at its center, flowing out to create great rivers and tributaries. Those tributaries overflowed, taking over the entire world until it was one solid, glistening ball of crimson.

A great evil laugh grew from a whisper to a scream. Max held his hands up to his ears and scowled.

"We don't know who or what removed the monster and its blight from the world. That happened before our time, but the legend was passed down through the orb of memory."

There was a bright flash, and the red globe was quickly replaced by a flickering blue ball. The light from within pushed away the darkness.

The screaming laugh of joyous evil changed to a shriek of pain.

"Then one day, a remnant of the blight took hold of a single witch. She traveled to the fae realm to perform an act of service for Queen Diaphne. A mission she swore an oath of secrecy about. We believe it was to find a relic otherwise lost to time.

Upon her return, we realized she had changed. There was a darkness in her, feeding on her very soul. When she tried to take the lives of her sisters, they trapped her with their magicks and performed the spells from the ancient Book of

Sins. A book created by the First Witch and left in our care for when the end of times came."

The orb spun round and round, faster and faster, until it exploded into a firework show of light. Blinding white and blue sparks lit up the sky.

When we regained our eyesight, we saw a woman with long red hair the color of blood and eyes the green of sapphires. Her dark skin was translucent and pearlescent at the same time. She wasn't human and didn't appear to be of fae blood either.

Something simultaneously between and yet more than either.

"It took the entire coven twelve full hours to remove the blight. Twelve brutal hours of fighting against the corruptive evil before they could pull our sister from the precipice of the darkness that consumed her. Two of our strongest did not survive."

The spell was abruptly broken by a knock at the door. We were all painfully wrenched back to reality. Star was nauseated by the sudden transition.

The normally festive, warm, and inviting room seemed dull and lifeless compared to the place they'd just been.

Another series of knocks came, this time in more rapid succession.

Max's jaw clenched in anger as he rose from the couch. His mug crashed to the floor, spilling its contents onto the polished wood as he rushed toward the door with a full-on feral growl.

Damn, that's hot!

"No! Don't answer it, Max." Mrs. Spigot spoke in a severe and commanding tone that took everyone by surprise. Gone were the cute giggles and sweetness. She sounded like a stern disciplinarian who found out you'd been sneaking out in the middle of the night to drink with college boys.

Duly reprimanded, Max slunk back to the sofa. Once he was firmly planted in his seat, pouting like a sulky child, Mrs. Spigot made her way to the door.

Before the door was even opened, Star knew who was standing on the other side. The magnetic draw of their bond seemed to know no distance.

Mrs. Spigot tugged on the doorknob harder than normal, almost as if the very house itself didn't want her to open it. Star was rooting for the door to win because she didn't want to face the person on the other side.

Creaaaaak.

"Hello. Pleasure to see you again. Mrs. Spigot, is it? May I come in?"

His French accent melted Star like butter. It took every ounce of her willpower not to scream "Yes," but the newest part of her, the one that had come to life just a few days ago, bolstered her strength.

She sat there quietly, staring into the contents of her mug.

Max growled again. Star could feel his muscles tensing without even looking at him.

How curious. Is it jealousy?

"No, I don't think that would be a good idea. I'll tell Star you came by, but she's busy at the moment and can't be interrupted."

"If you'll just invite me in, I can wait for her."

"No, I will not invite you in." Mrs. Spigot lowered her voice. The next word she said rang out into the night, making the hairs on the back of everyone's neck stand up at attention. "Vampire."

Chapter Twenty

Amira

"Vampire?" I whispered to Star. To say I was confused would be the understatement of the century. Yeah, I was aware of fairies, and I *was* a witch, after all. My incredulousness after our jaunt in Mrs. Spigot's dream story was naïve, even for me.

Star's eyes went wide. Apparently, she didn't know she'd been "dating"—term used loosely—a creature of the night. I guess that made sense. Not that I knew much about vampires other than what I'd read in horror novels back in high school. One thing I remember from my fiction: they could draw people toward them. I suppose not having that ability would make feasting on their victim's blood a lot harder to manage. No doubt a byproduct of spending most of their time being sexy.

I had to hold back a laugh.

The back of Florebelle's hand was pressed to her mouth. It looked like she was about to puke on Mrs. Spigot's immaculately clean wooden floor.

171

Despite not knowing much about vampires, I was now aware of the fact they couldn't enter a house without an invitation. That might not even necessarily be true, because *all* supernatural creatures had to be invited into the Witch's House.

We'd learned that during our last stay. Our concept of supernatural creatures had basically been limited to only fae at that point in time.

What else is out there?

I felt the deepening frown lines as my brows knit together. The ball of anxiety rising up, yet again. I could hold it together like no one's business in the courtroom, but not here, confronted by ancient evils and vampires lurking outside our front door. Vampires who seemed to have a deeply vested interest in my bestie, Star.

Not cool.

I don't think I was the only one in the room who could say they were pretty much over the drama.

Every time we came to this town, there was some kind of life-threatening tragedy or other. Why couldn't we just go back to that first day? We were blissfully ignorant when we'd spent the day downtown perusing the local shops. How nice it was to enjoy visiting our best friend to celebrate her birthday with complete and utter ignorance about the supernatural world around us.

Nice? Or boring?

The door slammed.

Max was up like greased lightning, headed to the nearest window. He pulled back the shade. Pretty sure he growled again.

What is up with that man?

"Well, it seems our brief interruption has caused a bit of a stir." Mrs. Spigot slipped right back into her normally pleasant self. Under other circumstances, her return to her usual state would have been a relief, but it proved too jarring and incongruent with the situation.

I need answers.

"He's a goddamned vampire?" Star wailed.

All eyes turned to her. She wasn't the type to cry or be histrionic. Star was the stoic, easygoing spirit. Our go-with-the-flow girl. But after what we had just gone through?

Star must be close to her breaking point.

Max abandoned his self-appointed post by the window and strode over to her. Putting a protective arm around her waist, he drew himself closer to her side. Maybe it wasn't just protection, maybe it was something more. I'd been picking up a distinct feeling from him since he showed up during what I could only call Florebelle's exorcism.

"Yeah, a goddamned vampire." His voice was sharp enough to cut through steel.

Silence.

We all waited for someone else to say something. Florebelle sat on the sofa beside Jareth. Her earlier nausea was worse, judging from the paleness of her skin and the light sheen of sweat breaking out on her brow.

Star broke free of Max and made her way to our barely recovered friend.

"Do you need more tea? How are you feeling?" She placed a hand on Florebelle's forehead. With her maternal instincts kicking in, she treated her like a child with a mean case of the flu. All thoughts of vampires or demons, the Book of Sins, weird memory bubbles, and witchery were pushed aside because of her concern for her Florebelle.

All I could think of was that I wanted to get the hell out of there. It was too much, too fast, and I wasn't equipped for this.

What I'd do to just be in a courtroom right now. I'd give

my left tit to be sitting at home reading a brief or hanging out in my beloved craft room surrounded by my sea of yarn.

Star

He is a vampire! A vampire? That explains so much, and so little, all at the same time. How could I not have known? Idiot. And Thibault, why didn't he warn me?

She shot a witheringly evil glance at her stalking specter.

She swore he could sense her thoughts, because he backed up several inches before ducking behind a grandfather clock near the door leading to the closest stairwell.

Screw this. Screw all of this!

Caught up by concern for Florebelle, she glanced over and saw her friend looking worse than earlier. Barely recuperated from the spell, the woman should be resting right now, not caught up in another big bag of crazy.

Maybe she needs another dose of my tonic. I should check for a fever.

"Do you need more tea? How are you feeling?"

Her forehead was cool and dewy. She was shivering like a newborn baby fawn.

"Maybe we should get some rest?" Mrs. Spigot's cheery voice brought us back.

"Yes. I, for one, vote for going to bed. I'm getting a little sick and tired of constantly being thrown into the crazy." Florebelle's voice was thin, but almost back to its usual volume and timbre.

"If we can just hold things together for a couple more days, maybe we can get out of this town relatively unscathed." Star couldn't help but laugh. Even to her own ears, her words rang hollow. "Okay, Jareth, can you get Florebelle settled while I go make her some more tea?"

She gave her friend a peck on the cheek and a quick cuddle before heading off to the one place in this colossal building that made her feel almost instantly at peace.

───────

When everyone had been recovering from their first run-in with the darker side of magicks and the evil Fairy Queen Diaphne, she'd wandered the house endlessly.

She'd gone from room to room, searching for something to take her mind off how they'd all nearly died. How her gift was wasted if she couldn't even protect her friends.

She'd opened yet another random door. This one led to a stunningly beautiful space of verdant green and pops of color, and the light filtered through stained glass.

You couldn't see this part of the building from the street as it was well hidden. And it was lovely. Every time she opened the doors to the conservatory, her heart skipped a beat.

The plants had been left to their own devices for years and their wildness was magickal.

Although they'd arrived in fall, it always felt like a warm spring day when she came here. There were some pockets where the temperature and light were cooler and darker. Convenient, because that was where most of the nightshade and mushrooms grew.

Star spent more and more time there. Whenever she could, in fact.

It tickles.

The sensation of leaves and flowers brushing against her skin when she walked past was titillating. A most delightful sensation. Especially when coupled with the sounds as they scraped and skipped across her clothes and skin, then whipped back to their original position.

No matter where you went, there was a distinctive scent that was stronger than the others. Here, the lavender was dominant. She pulled the small pair of clippers from the leather satchel at her waist—always kept there, just in case—and snipped a few flowers.

"For sleep, healing, and protection. Yes, this will do nicely."

Some would go into Florebelle's tea, but she had the inkling she might do a little something for the rest of the house. Something to help everyone get a good night's sleep and add an extra layer of shielding.

Every bit helps.

She made her way to the water feature. A small waterfall. Star still couldn't figure out where the water was coming from—set toward the back of the room, far away from the door. It almost looked like a shrine. The constant soft flow of water hitting water lulled her into a peaceful state of lucid dreaming.

She was surrounded by roses, high grass, and trees. The warm sun beat down while a cool wind blew in fleeting gusts. A refreshing counterpoint. The breeze almost sang to her. The time of day was early morning, by her estimation. She figured as much because she could see dewdrops on the petals of the roses.

"Star?"

She was so surprised, she dropped the lavender, tripped over her own feet, and nearly fell into the pool of water inches away. Her hand reached out and grabbed a white marble altar. In the process of saving herself, she knocked down several seashells.

Star heard the sharp crack as one of the shells broke.

"Oh shit. Sorry."

It was Max, sheepish and embarrassed.

She could feel the heat coming off him. He was silent like a predator stalking its prey—when he wasn't growling at vampires. Star hadn't heard him sneak up on her.

Either he'd figured out a way to bypass the inevitable creaky door that led into the conservatory, or she'd been completely entranced in her waking dream.

"Don't apologize. I was just daydreaming."

He bent over to pick up the spilled shells, reverently cradling the broken one. The crack hadn't broken it altogether. Star admitted that the black fault line didn't take away from the beauty of the piece. It was a thing to be admired. He set them back on the altar, touching each one gingerly with his fingertips, as if offering a silent apology. "Everyone went to bed. I thought I'd come see if you needed any help."

"No help needed." His sheepish look returned. "But I could definitely use the company." He perked back up.

Poor guy is probably being stoic. All the talk of vampires and the incantation from a few days back had to have put him on edge a little. Though he's handling it surprisingly well.

"Actually, I could use your help. Do you know what hoya is? I need three drops of nectar and a handful of petals."

Max pushed his sleeves as far up his muscular arms as he could manage, cracked his knuckles, and gave a jaunty wink. "Ask and ye shall receive."

He sniffed once and made his way straight to the hoya.

Hmmmm, seems he knows his way around this conservatory almost better than me! We'll make quick work of this!

Max and Star had a wonderful time together. With his help, she whipped up Florebelle's tea, assembled a cleansing wand, and made some Van Van oil—better to be safe than sorry.

The Van Van oil was a product of her days in New Orleans, studying under a great conjure doctor of much repute. The oil was used for all manner of things. Multipurpose, it was particularly great at getting rid of evil, changing bad luck to good luck, providing significant defense against magicks, and bolstering the strength of other charms.

Star was pretty sure Mrs. Spigot had more than a few charms lying around this enormous house. They were going to need all the help they could get.

Thoughts of the Hoodoo arts usually brought her back to her glorious stay in New Orleans, where she spent about two years off and on in the Gullah Geechee Nation. That was where she learned almost everything she knew about the traditional healing arts. She'd never be able to express the gratitude and love to that community for accepting her and treating her like family.

It was there, in fact, that a little old woman—ninety-five years old, to the day—made Star realize she might not actually be as crazy as she'd been led to believe.

"Why's that little demon following you around like a puppy?" the old woman said in Geechee. Star was barely fluent and quite confused by her question.

Usually, she stood out like a sore thumb, so people reverted to English when they spoke to her.

The older woman barely glanced up from her weaving—a sweetgrass basket—her deft fingers moving fast as lightning as she rocked away in a weathered old rocking chair.

"That demon. He been with you your whole life, hasn't he?"

The older woman's head tilted up so that Star got a good

look at her eyes, pupils a faded rheumy blue with specks of silver. She was blind.

"You can see him?"

"Clear as day. Which is funny, since I can't see nothin' else." She erupted into an infectious belly laugh. When both of them regained their composure, Star realized Thibault had stepped out of the shadows to stand right beside the old woman. This was the first time he'd been acknowledged in several years. Star had grown quite adept at ignoring him.

He leaned over and whispered something into the woman's ear. She sat up ramrod straight and nodded once, sharply, then went back to her weaving.

Now I felt like the invisible one.

By the time Star returned to the present from her trip into the realm of memories, she and Max had made their way to the kitchen. She pulled out the copper teapot, filled it, and set it on the stove to boil.

Max brought her two teacups.

"If this is a sleeping draft, I think Jareth could use some too. He hasn't slept in days. He can handle the lack of sleep, but I can't. It's either knock him out or I move to a room on the other side of the house. His nonstop pacing is driving me batshit crazy."

"Poor Max. Why do I have a feeling you get all mad and growly when you don't get your beauty rest?" Star winked and turned to her mortar and pestle. "Two steaming servings of knockout juice coming right up. Would you like to order anything else, sir?"

"Maybe you should make that three? I'm not sure I'll be able to sleep that well myself with your little friend in town."

Awkward.

Star didn't respond and just went back to assembling the ingredients for the tea in silence.

Most of the ingredients were fresh, but a couple of things were dried.

Maybe, in a few days, I could make some tea balls and take them down to Thyme and Treasures to see if Astra would be interested in selling them.

She adored the town shop, which sold gems and stones of the witchy variety, and imagined there must be a market for herbal remedies. Besides providing a service for the inhabitants of the area, it would be a great way to make a little extra pocket change to fund her next grand adventure.

"Could you pass me the honey, honey?" she asked playfully. The discomfort over Max's prior comment was long gone.

"Happy to oblige."

Within seconds, he was silently padding his way over to her with a mason jar of local honey. When his arm shot out to place the jar on the counter beside her, a startled Star dropped the pestle.

"You have *got* to stop doing that. Make a bit more noise, will ya? You're going to give me a heart attack!"

They chuckled as Star went back to preparing her sleeping draft.

Chapter Twenty-One

Amira

I didn't even realize I'd fallen asleep until a knock woke me up. Temporarily confused about where I was and scared that bad news was brewing, I jumped up and scrambled to the door so fast, my sheet was left trailing behind me on the floor.

On the other side was a looming Max and a cheery Star.

"Sorry if I woke you. Just wanted to smudge the room."

A few spicy words almost came out before I thought better of it and sleepily stomped down the hallway.

Star was being Star.

Probably never occurred to her that the time difference, chaos, and general exhaustion might mean she could smudge my room at a more reasonable hour. With a parched throat, I made my way to the kitchen for a glass of a beverage much stronger than water. Hopefully, the chef kept a little something-something around for sauces.

Surely they won't notice or mind if I have a shot or two.

Standing in the kitchen, I rubbed my eyes and wondered if I might still be fast asleep, dreaming in my bed.

The telltale signs of Star's messiness were quite clear, but an invisible force was cleaning up. A mortar and pestle dumped its contents into a small white ceramic bowl, then was wiped clean and placed back on the counter next to the stove.

A teapot drifted through the air, making its way to a tidy wooden shelf conveniently located right above the now-sparkling mortar and pestle.

Bits and bobs danced through the air; a broom swept into a dustpan to collect the detritus of her latest concoction.

"What the living hell?" I said into the empty air.

"Ahhh, the house feels comfortable with you lot now. She's willing to share her secrets." Mrs. Spigot placed a hand on my arm and gave a reassuring squeeze as she brushed past me. "You know how people have self-cleaning ovens? Well, we have a self-cleaning kitchen!" She chuckled heartily at her own joke.

"This place is cuckoo bananas. You know that, right?"

"Well, it *is* called the Witch's House, my dear. Would you like a cup of tea?"

"I was actually looking for something a little stronger."

"Hmm, think there's something here that will do the trick."

Mrs. Spigot opened a cabinet full of commercial-sized containers of herbs and spices.

"That won't do. No, not one bit."

She closed the door, then tapped on it three times. When she opened it again, it was a full-on liquor cabinet.

182

"So, does that kind of thing happen with all the cabinets in this house, or is it just that one?" I asked with incredulity.

"Pretty much anything in the house. You can ask it for clothes, alcohol, board games. Don't ask it for a gentleman caller, though. We had one witch do that facetiously. Let's just say things didn't go well. We had to erase the poor man's memory. He was never quite the same."

I giggled at the joke.

Or was it a joke? Who even knows at this point? It seems like anything is possible in the Witch's House.

Anything the imagination and a good spell book could come up with could be made real. That thought was both exhilarating and frightening at the same time.

With drinks poured, we sat down to chat. I brought the cut glass with a finger or two of amber liquid to my lips and took a long, deep sip.

Manna from heaven. Brandy, by my estimation. I'm not even a brandy lover, but this stuff really hits the spot.

"What brought you down to the kitchen looking for libations? Or do you not want to talk about it?"

"No, I'd rather not." I stared into the bottom of my glass. "But, I probably should." Mrs. Spigot observed me with gentle eyes. There was no judgment, only concern and genuine interest.

Opening up to people wasn't my strong suit. Mrs. Spigot waited patiently for me to gather my thoughts and speak. She radiated loving grandma vibes.

"Everything that's happened since we first set foot in Orphic Cove has been pure craziness. Overwhelmingly chaotic. I've known I was—" I hesitated, unsure how to continue without sounding strange. This was no courtroom. I could speak my mind, so I barged on, secure that in this moment, I was free to be myself. "My adopted family told me

I was a witch from a very young age, but my powers weren't as strong as theirs. I didn't feel like I fit in very well. When I was a teenager, I decided my path lay elsewhere. So, I went to college to become a lawyer. I live a damn great life. One most people would be proud of. I have my job and my yarn and I'm more than comfortable, but whenever I come here, it's extremely *un*comfortable, dangerous, and..." My eyebrows crinkled as I finally said what I'd been afraid to admit to myself for so long. "I'm starting to like it. The danger, I mean."

Picking up my glass, I drained it dry after my revelation. "Why do I like it?"

"Maybe you're just sick and tired of being comfortable. You have a destiny, you know? All three of you have great, big, powerful destinies."

I laughed drily at the thought of having a destiny that starts after reaching forty years old.

"Do you have a destiny, Mrs. Spigot?"

Her face became wistful and sad. "I had a destiny once and have it on good authority I'm not quite done yet." She snapped back to the moment with a twinkle in her eye. "I had charges. Been monitoring them their entire lives. Looking after them, keeping them safe, until the day they would find their own purposes. Their tale's still being written, but I do what I can, whenever I can, because, deep in my heart, the danger and chaos and all that goes with it—well, it's just life. And live we must. Until the day we die!"

She raised her glass, eyes firmly fixed on mine. I couldn't help but raise my mysteriously refilled glass in return.

"To destiny," I said to her.

"To destiny."

I slept like a baby that night, apart from waking up a couple of times in a coughing fit because of the fragrant remains of the smudge stick Star had burned earlier.

Really hope it doesn't make my clothes stink like a forest fire for the rest of my trip.

All I had was the outfit I wore here and a borrowed night-gown from Florebelle.

With a grunt of effort, I reached for my phone to check the time.

"Thirteen messages?"

The bad habit I'd developed over the years of checking my cell before getting out of bed and doing my morning ablutions reared its ugly head. This time, it was worth it, though, as my sleepy brain finally woke up and grasped that something big was blowing up at work.

Blowups at a legal office were never good.

By the looks of it, I was going to have to fly back to Seattle today. Due to all the magickal shenanigans over the past few months, I was fast running out of vacation days and excuses.

You could only kill off so many fake relatives before the higher-ups get suspicious or wonder if you had bad genes.

"Shit."

Ten of the thirteen messages came directly from the part-ners themselves. Long story short, they needed me back. Now.

The other three were from Carter. He was concerned because he hadn't seen me in the office and offered to bring over some chicken noodle soup if I was sick.

Our little tryst must have really rocked his world, because he'd turned into quite the attentive sweetie pie. Rehashing some of the finer memories of our night together made me smile.

I could definitely use a lot more "stress relief" like that in my life.

———

"I have to head back to Seattle ASAP. My phone's blowing up with texts from work."

"I have some good news," Star said, uncharacteristically chipper at this hour. A notorious night owl, mornings weren't kind to her, which typically made her not kind to *us*. This was a pleasant change. "Alexandre's gone. At least the helicopter is. He took off early this morning."

"Early this morning? Wouldn't that present a problem for a vampire?"

Star's eyebrows knitted together in thought. Apparently, I'd made a compelling point she hadn't quite considered.

"Yeah, that *is* kind of weird."

"Well, either way, he's gone. That's what matters. Good riddance, and huzzah!"

Florebelle eyed me quizzically. "Huzzah, Amira? You've never said that word in your entire life. Are you drunk?"

She was recovering nicely and in rare form.

"I may have had a tipple with Mrs. Spigot last night."

"Tipple, now? You know that trip to the Elder times wasn't real, right? I swear, woman. You need help." She gave me side-eye. Her glass hit the table a little too hard, spilling her orange juice on impact.

"Eldritch Times," I corrected her. The new look she shot my way made me swiftly change tack. "Um, did you know the kitchen cleans itself?" I asked. "Do you think the food cooks itself too?"

Star and Florebelle looked at me like I had grown a third eye.

"I swear! I came down looking for a drink when I saw things flying in the air. Dishes washing themselves. A broom was sweeping like in that Mickey Mouse movie. It was crazy. Mrs. Spigot even made a joke about it." I leaned in closer to the center of the table, whispering my next words. "I wonder if the butler's even a real person."

Florebelle cleared her throat, shaking her head from side to side so imperceptibly, I almost didn't notice, but it was too late.

"A real person, ma'am?" he asked from behind me. Sneaky little bugger had crept up with a tray full of tasty little tidbits.

I was not amused.

"I mean, of course you're real. Aren't you?" I asked, my face getting hot from the embarrassment of being overheard.

Instead of answering, he pulled the domed lid off the tray and served us our eggs Benedict in silence. That only made me more curious.

There was always some secret to be revealed here at the Witch's House.

———

Max was kind enough to drive us to the airport.

Surprise, surprise, Star sat in the front passenger seat.

It was hard not to laugh when he surreptitiously glanced over at her out of the corner of his eye when he thought she wasn't looking. He was going to end up another notch in her bedpost if we'd stayed much longer.

"I can't believe you two are leaving me again," Florebelle whined dramatically.

"Are you kidding? I offered to buy you a ticket three times since breakfast. I figured you'd cave when Star said she was coming back with me. You know I've got you, girl. Any time you need to leave Bad Juju Cove, all you need to do is call. I may not be a vampire with a fancy helicopter, but I can fly you out first class."

Star kept quiet. That was the first sign something was up. Normally, I'm pretty good at picking up on her signals, but let's just say I was surprised when we arrived at the airport to find Jareth standing there holding two bags.

"What the hell?" I asked as I turned to Florebelle for an explanation.

"Surprise! We're coming for an extended visit. Don't worry, we're bunking with Star. Everyone decided it was high time to get the heck out of Dodge for a bit. Besides, I've missed way too many girls' nights." Florebelle flashed an impish grin before opening the door.

"You coming too, Max? The more the merrier?" The sarcasm in my voice was thick as hospital oatmeal.

"Actually, I am."

"What?" My eyes had to be bulging out of their sockets. *Why is he coming to Seattle?* "Actually, don't answer that."

The five of us passed the time with idle conversation while waiting for Max to park the car and make his way back to us. It was refreshing, just talking like old friends about nothing of any relevance or great importance.

No weird tales of demons past or discussions about how to save ourselves from imminent danger, or free a relative stranger from certain death. Just a good ole normal conversation. It was refreshing.

And boring.

Star and I sat next to each other in first class. Everyone else was back in coach, so we ended up reconvening at the baggage claim area after landing, shooting the shit until the last bag was picked up.

When the rideshare car pulled up, I was left standing all alone.

As soon as I set foot in my condo, I headed for the shower, leaving a trail of clothes from the front door to the bathroom.

Restored and invigorated after washing all the crazy of the past few days off me, I put on a sharp suit and made my way to the office. That was when the shit really hit the fan.

It was going to be a long night.

"He's dead?" I was in shock.

Apparently, dropping his daughter off with his ex-wife had been Mr. Price's final act before overdosing on a bottle of pills.

None of this added up.

The man had more money than God and deeply cherished his own life and power. At least that was the persona he exuded whenever I was forced to be in a conversation with that slippery eel of a man.

I remembered him sitting back in his chair, smiling like a velociraptor, arms casually crossed over his chest as his lawyer announced they were leaving Susan with nothing, not even her daughter.

There was no way that man committed suicide. And if he did, it would be something a lot more ostentatious than downing a bottle of pills washed down with liquor.

Completely speechless, I stood there dumbfounded as George Wins himself told me the details of what our next steps would be.

Apparently, Price had also changed his will at the last

minute, giving the contents of his entire estate to his ex-wife and daughter.

He'd finalized the changes with his lawyer less than twelve hours before his suicide. The partners expected push-back from the other ex-wives and a spurned child from a previous marriage who received nothing. They wanted to make sure we had all our ducks in a row in case anyone contested the brand-new will.

Looked like this was going to be a long night. Price was a prominent man with a lot of influence. Not only was this going to be a newsworthy event, but our law firm was going to be at the center of it all.

Isn't this convenient? We lose the case, and a week later, he drops his daughter off, gives both his ex and daughter every-thing he has, and offs himself? No, not likely.

Chapter Twenty-Two

Amira

The rest of the afternoon went better than I'd hoped. I temporarily dropped any misgivings I had about Mr. Price and moved on to taking care of business. I got so absorbed in the minutiae, I almost didn't notice Carter's knock.

With a brain full to the brim of checklists and legal precedents, his visit was a pleasant distraction.

Well-timed too, because I'd been completely absorbed. I needed to wrap things up soon if I wanted to get a workout in before the gym closed. My plan: work out, plop in front of the loom, and lose myself in my yarn for at least a couple of hours before bed.

I waved him into my office, excited to have a pleasant conversation before packing up and heading home.

"Hey, hope I'm not bothering you." Carter swung the door open wide with one hand resting on the knob. He observed me with rapt attention. "You seem different."

"Different? Not that I know of." I saved a document and

locked my screen. "You're not bothering me. You actually have perfect timing. I'm about to head out for the day."

"Oh, good. I was too. Just wanted to stop in and say hello. Haven't seen you in a few days."

Is he fishing?

"Yeah." I waved a hand casually, as if brushing away his concern. "Just had a minor family emergency to attend to. It was unexpected and involved." I suddenly remembered I'd completely blown off his text. "Oh, Carter." My shoulders slumped, and I felt guilty as sin. "I never got back to you. Did I? Sorry. Family, you know?" I shrugged lamely.

He nodded, eyes warm with understanding. He took a step toward me with a look of rapt concentration that brought heat to my cheeks, among other areas.

The last time he'd looked at me so intensely, there'd been nothing between us except a thin layer of sweat from our exertion.

Maybe I should forget about the gym and have a different kind of workout tonight?

"You seem more..." He paused midsentence. I heard the soft babbling of coworkers as they moved closer to my door. "Well, just—more. Anyways, I'll let you finish up." Carter averted his gaze, looking as embarrassed as I felt. He turned to leave my office.

"Umm, thank you?" It came out as a question instead of a statement because I wasn't sure how to take what he'd said. Before he got past the doorframe, I blurted out an explosion of words: "I was about to head to dinner. Do you want to join me?"

He stopped in his tracks.

"Sure. I'd love to."

"Sushi?"

He grinned from ear to ear. "I love sushi."

"One of the best perks of living on the coast. I could eat the stuff three times a day and never get sick of it. Favorite sashimi?" I quipped as I closed the lid of my laptop.

"Hmm." His face scrunched up adorably while he pondered the question. "I honestly can't think of anything I don't like."

"Me neither."

"Oh, quick question for you. What kind of sushi restaurant would a lawyer open?"

"Uh, I don't know," I said in genuine confusion as I slid my laptop into its bag.

"A restaurant called Sosumi." He slapped at his taut, rock-hard thigh and laughed like a thirteen-year-old boy.

I couldn't help but join in.

"Oh. You've got jokes now, huh?" I slipped the latches of the laptop bag together with a click, then slung it over my shoulder. "You keep that up and I'm taking back my offer for dinner. Come on, funny man. Let's go get our sushi on."

Gasping and exhausted, I rolled off Carter and collapsed on the cool sheets.

My breath came in long, ragged gasps.

After another toe-curling marathon session, I knew I needed to head home soon if I wanted any chance of getting any sleep at all.

The man was insatiable.

"Wow!" Carter huffed as he reached over and dragged me close for a cuddle. He wrapped me in his arms and swung a well-formed, powerful leg over mine.

"Carter, tonight was amazing, but I have to go. Some friends are coming over."

He was silent, breathing slow and steady.

Is he asleep? Damn, I'm either going to have to slowly extricate myself from this human Jenga puzzle or gnaw off my own body parts if I want to go anywhere.

Star had texted me while we were at the restaurant to tell me, in no uncertain terms, I was hosting a brunch.

"Yeah, sure. I get it." He was hesitant to pull away. Our bodies were locked together so long, I thought he might have drifted off, but no. He pulled up his leg, giving me a quick squeeze, and nuzzled the back of my neck. His five-o'clock shadow tickled my sensitive skin in a way that was very arousing.

Before I got too far down the path of pondering if we might go for yet another round, he pulled back with a petulant sigh and swung his legs over the side of the bed, sitting there, cloaked in darkness. "You know, you could leave a few things here if you wanted."

I could only see his back, muscles tense.

"Maybe that's not a bad idea. Can we talk about it tomorrow?"

"Yeah." He stood and made his way to the bathroom while I fumbled for my belongings.

Once he left the bathroom, I went in. When our paths crossed, he paused. I stopped as well. He gently brushed my cheek with the backs of his fingers.

"You have the most beautiful voice I've ever heard."

What an odd compliment, but I'll take it. Not like the guy didn't recently worship the rest of my body. Repeatedly.

I stood on my tiptoes to kiss him, stopping right before our lips touched. "Do you mean my regular speaking voice? Or is this a moaning reference?"

He chuckled softly before coming in for the kill.

The man was making it extremely difficult to leave, but I

pulled away, breathless and tingly, before playfully pushing him backward with my hand on his chest.

With mock surprise, he took a step back and pretended to stumble before heading back to the bedroom. He stopped once to make sure I was enjoying the view before half turning to give me a saucy wink.

Once I'd made myself presentable, he walked me outside.

Ever the gentleman, Carter stood next to me on the sidewalk, waiting for my ride. We didn't say much.

We didn't have to.

Ours was a peaceful, comfortable silence that seemed to end all too soon.

"Construction? At this hour?"

The driver didn't realize it was a rhetorical question. "Yeah. I'm real sorry. Can't seem to get past the barricades." He seemed confused about what to do.

We were about five blocks from my condo, having driven in circles trying to find an open street that would lead us closer.

"It's okay. Just let me out here and I'll walk the rest of the way."

"Are you sure?" he asked, obviously concerned about his rating and his tip.

Okay, Miss Cynical, maybe he actually cares about the safety of a lone woman walking around at a late hour in a darkened neighborhood.

"I'll be fine. Thanks!"

Before I knew it, I was striding down the sidewalk on my way home.

Pain!

Something hit the back of my head. Before I could react, I saw the sidewalk coming up toward my face.

The fall was so sudden and gravity defying, it didn't seem like I was falling at all. The universe went all topsy-turvy.

Darkness.

"Amira, was it?" A familiar voice called my name in the dark. I tried to stand, but realized I was bound to a chair.

What the hell?

The sound of a snake slithering along a dry surface chilled me to the bone. I felt a breeze of cold air hit the back of my neck.

Did this fucker kidnap me?

"Alexandre?" The only French accent I'd heard in months, outside a subtitled art-house movie Star forced me to watch three months back, was pretty easy to identify.

Obviously, I was in a place where no one could hear me scream, because he hadn't bothered to gag me. Goddess knew where I was. This dude was rich enough to own a helicopter.

The world was still fuzzy, and my tongue was thick.

"I need water."

"Soon enough, ma petite." I could almost hear him smiling behind me.

One of those villainous grins where everything looks normal until you hit their cold, dead eyes. The sinister smile that chilled you to the bone.

He probably looked a lot like that snake right about now.

Alexandre pressed against me. I felt the chill from his body as he relaxed against the back of the chair, letting his mass push me forward several inches. The wooden legs emanated a high-pitched squeal that, under normal circumstances, would have made me cover my ears to block out the sound.

Since I was bound, I couldn't move.

Then I heard him huffing behind me.

"Are you sniffing my fucking hair?" I asked, more exasperated and disgusted than afraid. He wasn't fazed one bit.

"You smell so delicious. The last time we met, I knew you were special, but now?" His voice faded away to nothing.

Sometimes it's best to keep your mouth shut, and this definitely felt like one of those times.

Did I bring this on myself by telling Mrs. Spigot I craved danger?

"It won't be long now. The others will come looking for you. They brought that filthy beast. He'll no doubt sniff you out."

He appeared in front of me in a poof of smoke, like a cheesy magician's trick.

If it hadn't been for my recent dealings with fairies and ancient magickal curses, I likely would have lost my shit, but my mind clamped down into lawyer mode. Compartmentalization sure came in handy at times like these. Hold the personal stuff in, assess the situation, and try to find the cracks —the loopholes.

I was in my element.

It was time to play the silence game.

Alexandre looked at me expectantly, as if I was supposed to respond to his prompt. When I didn't play his little game, he continued speaking, the frustration evident in his voice. "Soon I'll have all three of you all to myself. Star already had a delightful darkness within her. She tasted of divinity. But now? It's grown a thousandfold. I could smell it on all of you in that damnable house."

Before I had time to react, not that it mattered with my

hands and feet bound as they were, the bastard latched himself onto my throat. His teeth sank deep into my flesh.

I wanted to scream, but something inside told me not to. Then, the same voice told me to pretend I was enjoying it. As idiotic as it felt, I started moaning.

After an eternity, he pulled back, hunger unsatiated. I could tell he wanted to drain me dry.

"Just a taste for now to quench the thirst. Once your friends get here, I'll have a most wondrous opportunity to possess more power than I could ever have dreamt of. I thought the L'i'al Dool to be an old wives' tale, passed down from generation to generation."

He danced about in glee. His face was flushed—most likely from consuming my blood full of power from the L'i'al Dool. He kept babbling, but I'd tuned him out. I'd had the power of the L'i'al Dool for all of five minutes and didn't know how to use it or I'd have blown this asshole to smithereens.

I stayed quiet and tried to make myself as small as possible, acting as if I were in a trance. I kept listening to that little voice inside that gave me instructions on what to do.

Drop your chin to your chest and close your eyes.

Lemme tell you... It's really hard to sit in a darkened room with a hungry vampire you're pretty sure wants to use you as bait—so he can eat you and your friends—and there isn't a damned thing you can do about it.

Time passed quickly. Perhaps I fell asleep from the blood loss. All I know is I almost jerked my head up in surprise when I heard Alexandre's voice from several feet away.

"They're here."

He was positively giddy.

"Not long now, and you'll all be mine. I'll drain you bitches dry and steal your power if it's the last thing I do."

Star

Star was concerned. With hours to go before everyone was supposed to gather for brunch, she snuck into her guest room to shake Florebelle awake.

"Huh? What? Are you okay? Did I oversleep?" Florebelle yawned and rubbed her eyes.

"No. Something's wrong." Star couldn't describe the intense jolt of danger that pulled her out of the most luscious dream. She was the Queen of Sheba, being attended to by an extremely attentive harem of men.

"Wrong?"

Jareth stirred at the sound of her voice.

"Yeah. I don't have any proof, but I think something's happened to Amira."

More awake now, Florebelle could think straight and form more than monosyllabic responses. "If it were anyone else, I'd say you were crazy, roll over, and go back to sleep, but if you think something's wrong, we should check on her. Have you called? She's usually awake by now."

"Yeah, I called and texted."

Jareth stood and made his way to the door. "I'll wake Max. He's probably just pretending to sleep anyway."

Florebelle scrambled to gather her clothes, putting her T-shirt on inside out without noticing. She scooped her shoes up and headed toward the bathroom.

Everyone was dressed, assembled, and ready to go in less than five minutes.

There were no telltale signs of construction when they arrived. The only hint of Amira's presence was a small rusty red spot in the middle of the sidewalk several blocks from her home.

A spot they would have completely missed if Max hadn't stopped dead in his tracks. It was so sudden, the others were halfway down the block before they noticed and doubled back.

"Did you find something?" Jareth asked with concern.

"Amira was taken," Max said under his breath as he further examined the now-dry evidence of Amira's presence. "It's that goddamned vampire. It positively reeks of him."

"Alexandre took Amira? Why would he do that? That doesn't make any sense. If he was trying to come after me, all he had to do was call and I'd come running." Star was ashamed. The words were bitter, hard truths she wasn't quite willing to face up to.

Except right here, right now, bathed in the spotlight of an unforgiving streetlamp in the early morning hours, she knew she had to admit the power he had over her.

She wasn't just admitting it to her friends and Max, she was admitting it to herself, out loud, for the very first time.

Her soul laid bare, she didn't like what she saw.

Not one bit.

Max turned on a heel and made his way down the pitch-black alley. The others followed. The beam from the streetlights barely penetrated the back street.

They were soon plunged into darkness.

Chapter Twenty-Three

Star

The impenetrable darkness overwhelmed their senses and made them feel like they weren't moving at all.

"Max, to me. Flora and Star, one of you grab Max, then hold the other's hand. Whatever you do, don't let go," Jareth ordered.

"Jareth, what's going on? Are you doing this?" Star's voice wavered. The most happy-go-lucky person in the group was on the verge of hysteria.

"Yes, sorry. I have to take us into the shadow realm. The vampire set up some kind of elaborate veil. It would lead us straight to him, but this is definitely a trap."

Florebelle's anger surged. "For chrissakes, light fae, dark fae, and now vampires? If we make it out of here, Mrs. Spigot is giving me witch lessons as soon as we get back to Orphic Cove. I'm sick of being defenseless."

Star hoped an angry Florebelle would be the very thing to save them. It had worked before, after all.

Her knees buckled, and she almost let go of Max's hand.

He gripped her harder. Not so hard as to be a crushing pressure, but hard enough to reassure her he wasn't leaving her behind.

Star regained her footing and walked off into the inky darkness with her usual swagger. She had a sudden jolt of energy that significantly improved her disposition.

Max slowed, drawing Jareth back.

"You okay, old friend?" Jareth asked. With the lack of light, he barely made out Max's expression of pain. His concern deepened. Max gritted his teeth and nodded resolutely.

They continued forward.

"Left."

"You sure, Max?"

"Yeah, left, then straight ahead."

"How are you doing this?" Star was more confident now, and her voice was much louder than before.

"Max is a tracker. A powerful one. He can even track scents through the shadow realm. It's one of the many reasons the Unseelie queen recruited him to work for us."

"Well, I was also adopted by your family and spent several years hanging out in the castle."

"Okay, that too. I did say many reasons."

The banter between the two men was uplifting though eerie, because their voices lacked the full range of sound the women were used to. Everything was deadened here. It was as if they were in a padded room that absorbed the upper and lower frequencies, leaving everything feeling dull and flat.

Star's head swiveled to the left. Despite the darkness, she could make out moving shadows. People had always said her night vision was impeccable, unnatural, but this?

This is absolutely crazypants. Seeing shadows in a shadow?

She almost piped up with a question for Jareth, but realized it was the wrong place, wrong time.

Star wasn't too keen on the fact several of those shadows appeared to be staring at her specifically. A few darted in close, almost within touching range. She sensed their curiosity.

How can a shadow be curious?

Jareth's voice cut through the stillness. "We're here."

They popped out in a warehouse the Goddess only knew where.

"Oh, hell no." Star didn't even try to keep her voice down. "Is this an abattoir?"

Carter

I followed the four strangers I heard saying Amira's name.

I'd texted her to let her know she'd left her laptop over at my place and offered to drop it off in the morning, but never heard back.

Part of me hoped if she got the text early enough, she might invite me over for the night. A silly thought, but worth a shot, nonetheless.

I couldn't get enough of her.

Hadn't been able to since the day I first caught her humming to herself in the break room. I felt myself breaking into a smile at the memory. Then, I heard the tall, muscular, dark-haired guy say Amira had been taken by a vampire.

I pulled out my cell phone from a back pocket and held it to my ear, pretending to concentrate, mouthing words just in case they looked over and saw me standing there watching them.

How close can I get without drawing too much attention?

I didn't want to lose them, but knew it was much more likely I'd get caught if I were following a bunch of strangers this early in the morning. There was no one else on the street at this hour.

The four ducked into the alley.

Thirty seconds. Then I'll follow them.

After waiting for half that time, my impatience got the better of me. I dashed across the street to follow them.

It didn't take long before I hit a wall. I could sense the magickal barrier and knew I couldn't pass through. Besides, it felt like a setup. The tickle at the back of my neck was proof enough of that. If there was one thing I was good at recognizing, it was a trap.

Backing away slowly, I realized the best I could do was wish Amira's friends good luck.

How am I going to figure out where they went?

There was one way. Something I'd sworn I wouldn't ever do again because it violated my ethical boundaries.

But desperate times...

Cloaked by the alley's darkness, standing in the same spot where the tall, burly, dark-haired man had been just moments before, I saw the maroon patch. Any hesitation over establishing my connection with Amira was shattered when I saw her blood.

I had no choice. Ever since the day I'd first laid eyes on her, I knew in my heart who it was I belonged to.

I closed my eyes and called out to her. "Amira... Amira..."

Within seconds, I knew exactly where she was.

My phone was out in an instant with the rideshare app opened. I plugged in an address I knew was close to the location where I sensed Amira was being held.

When I relaxed my mind and called out to her, I always

knew exactly where she was, but it had been years since I'd used that power.

It felt like an infringement on her autonomy.

———

Less than twenty minutes later, I stood in front of an abandoned complex on the outskirts of the city.

Dark, dingy, and dangerous.

I'd asked the driver to ride around the block a few times in order to get a feel for the area before having him let me out a few streets over. Scoping out the place made me feel like a spy on an espionage mission, but this was no time for games. I had to figure out what I was going to do.

My connection to Amira hadn't been completely extinguished, though I'd loosened it, so to speak. The mere thought of dropping it completely and potentially never getting it back made my heart race.

Right now, my biggest concern was her getting hurt—or worse, but there was no major change in her physical or emotional state. As far as I could tell, she was in relative peace.

When I walked up to the chain-link fence surrounding the property, I could almost hear her gentle snoring. That normally would have made me smile, but now it had the opposite effect.

I'll kill whoever's done this to her.

Trying to stay hidden while figuring out if there was a break in the fence brought me back into focus.

Success!

There was a small section of the fence's chain that had been snipped, and no telltale tickle at the base of my neck—a good sign. If all went well, I was home free. If not, I was completely screwed, because the only other way into the building was through the front door.

And doing something as rash as that likely wouldn't help anybody.

Within minutes, I was hiding behind a giant pile of old tires, which reeked of mold and mildew. It made a great place to hide while I contemplated my next steps.

CLICK!

I heard the sharp sound inches away, directly on the other side of the tires. Crouching down with my breath held for a full three minutes, I didn't dare to move a muscle.

I can't get caught now...

My body tensed as I heard footsteps closing in on my hiding place. There was nowhere for me to go if they came around to my side. I'd have to defend myself with my back against the wall of the decrepit building.

Not very good odds.

Static. "Lars! Check the A wing. Boss says we're expecting company."

"A wing confirmed," the man named Lars said from only three feet away before sauntering off at a snail's pace in the opposite direction.

My heart only stopped racing after I peeked around the edge of the giant rubber mound. I saw the back of the guard as he rounded a corner and walked out of sight.

I crept forward, nervous to leave the protective mound of tires that had just saved my ass, but I pressed on until I reached a door at the side of the building.

I'm so close, I can smell her.

Star

Alexandre and several minions were waiting for them once they popped out of the shadows.

Jareth, Max, and Florebelle made their way out into the light, with Star taking up the rear. She was more than eager to get away from the creepy silhouettes reaching for her and wasn't about to find out if they wanted to drag her back into the shadow realm with their curious, barely there wisps of fingers.

Perhaps that fate would have been better for what was undoubtedly going to befall them, because the first thing she saw after her eyes adjusted to the light was Alexandre, looking mighty hangry.

He eyed the two women like they were a couple of mouth-watering Thanksgiving dinners being handed to him on a silver platter, and he was about to dig in.

Then ask for thirds and fourths.

"Take them into the other room," Alexandre ordered his lackeys.

Max pounced.

Florebelle's and Star's eyes opened wide as saucers when they saw him clear nearly fifteen vertical feet—his descent clearly aimed at Alexandre. At the last moment, Max smashed into an invisible wall with a sickening crunch, bouncing backward like a rubber ball before collapsing onto the ground.

"Anyone else want to try anything?" Alexandre gave each of his captives a look that made them think twice about their next move. Jareth slipped back into the shadows. *Dammit*, Alexandre mouthed before waving someone forward.

The woman who strode to his side was almost seven feet tall and built like a brick shithouse and decked out in a close-fitting black satin dress that looked like it came from a 1950s pinup calendar. She was vintage and sexy, wearing expensive velvet high-heeled shoes. The woman slipped on elbow-length black latex gloves and casually strolled over to the spot Jareth had just disappeared into.

The dark-haired vixen reached her right arm into the shadow elbow-deep. The next sound they heard was a sucking pop, followed by thrashing and a muffled scream. Her raised arm quivered right before there was a loud rip like someone was tearing wet cotton broadcloth.

As she backed away from the shadow, Jareth was dragged back into the room.

"Meet Elmirath. Your little shadow-walking friend has nothing on her. She can reach into anything and find the thing she seeks. Nifty little power, eh? Especially when one loses one's car keys in the middle of the night."

Elmirath chuckled as she dragged Jareth by the throat over to Alexandre.

His face was blue. Elmirath's viselike grip made Star afraid the witch had the strength to crush his larynx. The only thing standing in her way was a single command from Alexandre. She shuddered at the thought and wrapped her arms around herself in a comforting hug.

After a deep breath, she relaxed, resolved in what she must do. Her arms fell to her sides. Her back straightened.

"Alexandre, let them go. Take me instead." Star commanded rather than pleaded.

"I will take you and your little friend. I will take you all. My men can play with the rest. Come here, my pet."

Star walked forward involuntarily.

She struggled against him, or whatever power was drawing her toward him against her will, but it was to no avail.

Confused, frustrated, and shocked, she slowly marched

right up to Alexandre's side and planted a kiss on his lips. She burned with desire for him. Her body fiercely craved something her mind rebelled against. The war didn't last long. Star's body won out.

This isn't the first time.

Star succumbed to the darkness.

Florebelle

"Star?" Florebelle's voice was barely above a whisper as she called her friend's name.

Her eyes shifted from Star to Jareth and then to Max. Florebelle backed away, unsure of how to proceed. Her fight and anger had melted away, replaced with fear. This was too much like the last time, when she was imprisoned by her evil stepmother. Stepfairy.

Star was trapped under a mind-altering spell, and here they were at death's door.

Florebelle laughed.

As inappropriate and nonsensical as it was, the thought of a stepfairy made her giggle uncontrollably.

She was still too weak to fight and saw no way out of this. They were surrounded by a powerful vampire, his witch, and dozens of his minions. Star was held transfixed in some kind of spell or was mesmerized. Jareth was being choked out by the witch, and Max was lying unconscious on the floor.

It was time to give up and accept her fate. Without her sisters or her rage, she couldn't retaliate, and she was so tired of fighting for her life every five minutes.

Maybe death would be easier?

One minion walked toward her. Florebelle stepped back,

laughing all the while until she felt the cool strength of a wall behind her back.

She felt a spark deep inside her. That spark became a flame. That flame became a raging fire. She stopped laughing and focused on that fire and thought of what she had to fight for.

"Oh no, none of that. I've been around hysterical witches and angry witches long enough to know that's when you make the most trouble," Alexandre said before moving toward her at the speed of light.

Within a split second, he went from being a blur to standing directly in front of her, hands firmly gripping her shoulders. His grip intensified. He was crushing her with his brute strength. One of his hands flew up to cup the side of her head, pressing it down so hard, her ear slammed into her shoulder.

Florebelle felt the sharp sting of his teeth penetrate her skin before she had time to fight him off.

Drifting. Drifting. It feels so good.

Alexandre moaned, coming up for air only after he had taken his long sip.

"Fucking fairies. Forgot how delicious you are." He wiped his mouth with the back of his hand.

"Tie them all up with the other one. We don't have much time."

———

Amira

By the time I woke up, all my friends were strapped into their very own chairs.

Once the half dozen of Alexandre's minions left us alone

and I no longer heard their footsteps, I figured it was safe enough to talk to my friends.

"Are you okay?"

Silence.

Not a peep out of anyone.

"Florebelle?" I waited for a response before speaking louder. "Star?"

Still nothing.

There was no way on the Goddess's green earth these two would be this quiet and not struggle against their bonds unless they were hog-tied, gagged, and roofied.

What did Alexandre do to them? And how are we going to get out of this alive?

BOOM! A paint can fell to the ground.

Chapter Twenty-Four

Carter

I was livid, positively seeing red once I caught a glimpse of Amira. Not only was she tied up and damned near unresponsive, but there wasn't anything I could do about it. Not until the thugs who had just arrived cleared out.

They brought the people I'd followed into the alley with them. Two women and two men, all of whom were unconscious. The men looked a little worse for wear.

The hoodlums tied her friends to chairs. It was a test of my willpower and fortitude to sit back and let them do what they wanted. The difficulty of maintaining restraint and not striding out like an idiot to beat their asses was contained by grinding my teeth to nubs. The muscles in my clenched jaw ached.

Bravado would get me nowhere. I rested against the sturdy shelf and bided my time. It provided great cover and kept me undetected while I lay in wait. At least two of the kidnappers, the older French gentleman and the insanely tall brunette, had magicks. And I was willing to bet that the

French guy was the vampire I overheard them talking about earlier.

That was one thing in my favor. I couldn't be mesmerized by them, and as long as we were in a room together, Amira's friends wouldn't be affected either.

My patience was wearing thin. I was about thirty seconds away from breaking out to make a rather mad and dangerous rush regardless of the consequences, but, just like that, the gods swung the trident of fate in my favor. All the vampire's minions cleared out, exiting the room like a chaotic swarm of killer bees.

"Are you okay?" Amira whispered to her friends.

Was she faking it the entire time? Had her slumped-over, loose, sloppy posture all been a façade? Why hadn't I sensed it?

Silence.

"Flora?" She paused. "Star?"

That was when I saw it. The bite mark on Amira's neck. My hatred of the vampire flared up and my hackles rose.

It's going to be hard to maintain the level of caution necessary to make it out of this vamp den unscathed.

I'd only had one up-close-and-personal experience with a vampire in my life, and it hadn't ended well. In fact, the only reason I survived was because the hosts of the party, Tim and Marsha, had hidden several guests in a panic room while they went in search of their daughter.

Tim was a coworker at the law firm, my first friend in Seattle. He'd invited me over for a friendly dinner with a few other couples when their daughter let a stranger into the house.

At the first sign of trouble, we were herded into their private safe room, but right before they locked the door, Tim and Marsha left to look for their daughter.

Everyone who hadn't been locked in with us died. Those

of us who survived saw a fraction of the bloodbath when the police unlocked the door and led us to the waiting ambulances.

None of us were considered suspects because there was a video log showing exactly when the door to the panic room was closed.

It never opened after it locked. Not until the cops showed up.

Tim and Marsha had saved our lives.

That was one dinner party I'll never forget. Tonight is likely to rank pretty high on that list. If we get out of this alive.

Carter smiled wryly as he inched closer. He froze when his elbow connected with an empty paint can. It went crashing to the floor far from the cheap metal shelf.

BOOM!

Idiot! All you need is for them to come in here with guns blazing.

Amira's head jerked around immediately at the sound of the can clattering to the floor. Her eyes nearly bugged out of her head.

"Carter?" Hearing my name as a whisper on her luscious lips was like music to my ears. Amira didn't look surprised or confused by my presence. She was annoyed. Surely, she'd forgive my transgressions once I freed her and her friends? Any questions about my presence here could be answered when we were all safe and sound.

Good thing I was the perfect Boy Scout, even though I'd never been clear on what exactly a Boy Scout did or even was. People had said that to me several times since I'd arrived in Seattle whenever I pulled out the right tool on a whim. Now, I fished out my Swiss army knife and cut through the cords binding Amira's hands and feet.

She rubbed her wrists, face scrunched up in pain as the circulation went back into her hands.

"We have to free the others. He must have done something to them. Alexandre's a—" She hesitated. "He's dangerous."

"Well, yeah. Understatement of the year. Vamps are deadly." I gave her a visual once-over before heading to the closest chair to free one of her friends.

"I think he's got control of them somehow."

Her statement sparked another memory. When I was in the panic room, a few of the people had talked about how Tim and Marsha's oldest daughter, probably around eighteen, had gotten up suddenly during our get-together and made a beeline for the front door.

To their knowledge, no one had knocked or rung the bell. She'd invited someone in when I was in the bathroom, sopping up marinara sauce I'd dripped onto my favorite tie.

She wore a scarf around her neck.

I'll always remember that scarf—blue silk with pink cherry blossoms on it. I remembered it because it didn't remotely match her outfit, something she was always meticulous about. So much so, it had become a small joke at the party.

If only I had been in the room, Tim and Marsha might still be alive.

"Well, we'd better free them and figure out how to snap them out of it. It's nearly dawn. Hopefully, he won't be able to control them when he sleeps. Or whatever vampires do during daylight hours."

The last person we freed was the dark-haired guy who looked like he could have broken through the skimpy rope with brute strength if he weren't unconscious, with blood dripping out of his nose.

Once the rope was cut and his hands unbound, his eyes snapped open. They flashed a bright neon green. His pupils looked freaky, but once I blinked, they went back to normal dark eyes.

Weird. I must be seeing things.

He made me uneasy.

"You're free, man," I said as I backed away, afraid the guy might still be in fight-or-flight mode from whatever had messed him up in the other room. His whole body shivered as if to release tension, then he stood up, flexed, and cracked his knuckles.

"Max," he said with a hand outstretched. I took it and he pumped it hard, once, so hard it almost yanked my arm out of the socket. "Thank you."

His eyes were sincere.

"Carter, and any time, but let's not make a habit of it. We might want to save any more friendly chat for after we get out of here. If we get out of here."

Max nodded, smirked, and immediately walked out of the room.

Max strode into the adjacent room with purpose and determination, then leapt on top of a stack of pallets ten feet high with the ease of an Olympian doing a cool down. He perched there, observing the men sitting at a cheap, rickety table playing cards.

There were a total of three men, and they were oblivious enough it might be fairly easy to dispatch them quickly. Max leapt onto a large metal shelf made of sturdier stuff than the room we had just left. He landed on it so quietly, the only thing that alarmed the men was the shadow that suddenly appeared over their card table.

They hurriedly grabbed the guns at their waists, fumbling and nervous as they jumped out of their seats.

A bald man with a '70s porn 'stache lost his balance and tumbled backward, breaking through the chair he'd just been sitting on. Unlucky bastard landed so hard, he cracked his head open on the unforgiving cement floor.

One down, two to go. The odds were slowly increasing that we'd get out of this unscathed.

Unrealistically optimistic much?

Max leapt on top of one of the remaining men, arms wrapped around his neck as he slid down his back with the fluid grace of a mutant spider monkey.

SNAP!

The man's neck broke, but Max held on as the remaining thug opened fire. He pushed the corpse he was holding forward with speed and precision. The body flew at the remaining henchman like a human-sized bullet, knocking him down under the mass and force of it all.

He tried to scramble out from under the body, but Max was too fast. He took two enormous steps—so large, it looked like he was flying across the filthy concrete floor, then launched himself several feet into the air, did a flip, and came down with his boot straight into the man's head.

Third guy down.

The alarm rang through the otherwise silent building, alerting everyone within that there was danger afoot.

More guards came, and one by one, Max easily dispatched them.

Everything was going well until the tall witch appeared.

She lifted a hand. Max flew back, landing hard against the

wall. I heard the hiss of an exhalation like a rapidly deflating tire, but that man was a fighter.

Even with the breath knocked out of him, he continued to battle against the crushing magickal force that kept his body firmly pressed against the wall, his feet dangling a foot or more off the ground.

Almost as suddenly as he was flung backward, he was pulled forward. Max slid to the ground. The ozone-tinged scent of dissipating magicks hung thick in the air.

The dark-haired witch lay on the ground. It was her turn to be passed out.

Amira stood behind her with a leg from one of the shattered chairs from the first round of amateur jailers in her hand.

A drop of blood slid down the wooden shaft and dripped onto the floor beside the witch's head.

Max gave a nod of approval. Amira returned the nod with a smile.

That was when the fun *really* began.

Star

Star wanted to cry, but she couldn't because she was trapped in her own body, her mind held captive in a dark place worse than the shadow realm. She'd take those creepy bastards with their curious fingers over what she was feeling now any day of the week.

Trapped and helpless, she was paralyzed and blind, caught up in the deep recesses of her mind as if floating in space, except she could feel her body around her. She wore it like an astronaut wears a space suit. This feeling was foreign to her. Star was no longer the master of her world.

I'm nothing more than a puppet on a string.

When the image of her puppet master popped into her head, she tried to scream. The fear and frustration over dragging her friends into a trap with no idea how to get out of it was too much. She was racked with guilt.

This is all my fault.

Whatever strength and power she'd found within the walls of the Witch's House after absorbing the L'i'al Dool wasn't enough to fight this.

Star thrashed against the darkness. The claustrophobia of being trapped in her own mind caused her to panic.

Max

Alexandre was visibly pissed, if the deep scowl and blobs of spittle forming on the corners of his mouth were any indication. Between the foam and his gnashing canines, he looked like a rabid dog in berserker mode.

He was a blur as he zoomed past his guards. There wasn't an ounce of fear in him. His senses, reflexes, and brute strength had likely been bolstered after he'd taken a few sips of the blood of his captives. Blood brimming with the ancient power of the L'i'al Dool.

Max had shaken off yet another potentially fatal altercation with Alexandre's passed-out witch.

The playing field was even now.

Without her magicks thwarting his natural abilities and defying the laws of nature, he had the speed, strength, and stamina to fight off an average vampire.

He might not be at full strength, but he was a formidable foe.

Unfortunately for him, he'd duly underestimated how much Alexandre had leveled up by consuming the L'i'al Dool.

With power and speed increased, the vamp levied a powerful uppercut with a speed Max couldn't avoid.

He flew backward, back hitting the sturdy metal shelving with an explosive crack. His vision doubled, but he shook it off, stood up, and went back for more.

Amira hummed.

The vampire's blinding speed slowed down significantly.

No matter how hard Alexandre fought, he became slower and slower until he came to a standstill, like an ant trapped in molasses.

Carter snatched the chair leg from Amira's hand and sprang forward as the first guard came closer. At the last moment, Carter pivoted, then threw himself backward, jamming the stake through the vampire's back.

A direct hit to the heart.

Alexandre collapsed, a look of shock and disbelief on his face.

All the strength and vitality born of his old age and the power of the L'i'al Dool seeped from his body. He withered before them like a time-lapse movie on some demented educational channel of a grape turning into a raisin.

He became gray stone, a bewildered statue, but he didn't crumble to dust. Only his panicked eyes remained alive and untouched until the rays of the new dawn's sun blasted through a window, covered him with its beams of light.

The stench of his seared flesh wafted through the air. It smelled of decay, burning paper, and cinnamon.

He burst into giant gouts of flames, whose blazes licked at Carter's toes when he stood a bit too close.

The minions looked on in horror, unsure of what to do next. Most of them broke ranks and fled. A few looked relieved, as if they'd been freed from some great burden.

Amira and Carter dropped into a fighting posture, ready to take on those who remained loyal to their master, but in the end, it was Star's scream from the other room that led the three to retreat from their position and run back to her.

Star

Star was racked by relieved sobs. Her scream rang out so loud and pure that it ripped through her throat. That pain was a blessing because it gave a confirmation she was back.

Back in her body. Back in the real world. No longer trapped in the shadows of her mind. A place that was a thousand times worse than the shadow realm Jareth had led them through.

Florebelle stared off into space, a look of pure confusion and dread on her face. Jareth stood on wobbly legs and went to her.

"No, check on Star," she said in a voice that was much too calm.

By the time he reached Star, Max, Amira, and Carter entered the room at a run. Max was far ahead of the other two, despite starting from several hundred feet farther away.

Amira made a beeline straight to Star.

"Star, sweetie, are you okay? Did he hurt you?"

"No, no. It was just so..." Star stopped, stood, and wrapped her friend in her arms.

Florebelle joined in, her gaze still miles away. "We didn't

die," she said dully into Amira's shoulder. Her tears soaked into the fabric of her friend's shirt.

After a few more tears of relief, comforting pats, and loving hugs, everyone made their way out of the building by going back the way Carter had come, sliding through the broken section of chain-link fence.

Once they were far enough from the building, Carter and Amira called for separate rideshare vehicles, both headed to her place. She was the only one who had enough room for everyone to stay over, and they didn't want to be separated.

Not tonight, at least.

Chapter Twenty-Five

Amira

Florebelle, Star, and I sat in silence all the way back to my condo.

I mean, what were we supposed to say with a stranger in the front seat who'd likely wind up telling stories for the rest of his life about the batshit crazy women he'd picked up who suffered from a mass delusion?

He'd probably blame it on drugs. And I, for one, wasn't going to allow that to go down no matter how much I wanted to talk to Star and Florebelle about what had just happened.

Star stared vacantly out the window, barely moving a muscle the entire ride. If it hadn't been for the bumps on the road, she'd have looked like a statue in gentle repose, eyes caught up in a ten-mile stare.

Florebelle immediately curled up next to me and fell asleep with her head on my shoulder. I couldn't blame her. After everything she'd been through, she'd never had a chance to fully recover from the L'i'al Dool before the next hot mess situation.

At least Star and I had more experience with magickal things in general, having been witches pretty much our entire lives. Florebelle only recently found out and had a trial by fire of epic proportions. An experience I wouldn't wish on anyone.

She wasn't the only one shell-shocked. Despite our being aware of magicks, neither Star nor I had encountered anything at this level before.

It was hard for me to process. Star was catatonic. I couldn't even fathom what was going through Florebelle's mind.

Speaking of minds, I couldn't help but wonder how hers was holding up.

We were all hijacked by the ancient curse of the L'i'al Dool, but I had a sneaking suspicion it affected Florebelle differently from Star and me. Perhaps that was because the ancient curse was so fresh in the two of us. Florebelle had been carrying it around for longer, but I didn't think that was the case.

I had a sneaking suspicion it went much deeper, and darker, than that.

But that was an issue for a different day. Today, I just wanted to get home, take a bath, and curl up in my bed sandwiched between my two besties, knowing we were safe...for today, at least.

Seemed like being on the verge of death, or possibly even worse, was all the rage for our little trio since our happy, little surprise birthday visit to Orphic Cove.

The driver pulled up to my place, where there was not a single construction cone in sight.

I knew that bastard had set the whole thing up.

With my suspicions confirmed, I gently pressed on Florebelle's shoulder. "We're here, Flo. Time to wake up."

She jumped. The light of recognition hit her eyes, and she smiled up at me.

"I just had the craziest nightmare." Her sentence was half caught up in a yawn and barely comprehensible.

"Let's talk about it inside." I opened the car door and slid out, waiting for Florebelle and Star to follow. Florebelle was hot on my heels, but Star just sat inside with that same faraway stare until Florebelle tugged on her arm and she finally exited the vehicle.

I knew I should be worried, but I was too tired and really didn't want to think about anything—good or bad—until we were safely together behind my locked front door.

Pulling out my key, I let my friends into the apartment and debated on going downstairs to wait for the boys. I thought the cool air might do me some good, but my head throbbed as if the pain wanted to remind me about what had happened the last time I was outside alone.

I made a solemn vow that last night's events wouldn't turn me into a quivering pile of jelly, afraid to walk down a city street at night. I was not some shrinking violet frightened of her own shadow just because one big, bad vampire decided to thunk me on the head and use me as bait to lure my friends so he could drain us dry and increase his power a thousandfold.

This was my house, my town, and I was one powerful witch—even more powerful when I was with my girlfriends. Besides, we'd made it through too many scrapes to even consider trying to hide for fear of the unknown.

Either way, I wanted a hot bath. With bubbles.

Tonight, I deserved the fancy bubble bath. The one I bought at the bougie store in Paris. Wasn't sure if it was actually tourist prices or just highbrow, but I was going to soak my troubles away tonight.

Pure luxury.

I deserved a moment.

"Shit, my bag."

I'd left my laptop at Carter's place. Pretty sure he didn't take it with him to the house of horrors.

Abattoir of horrors.

I chuckled to myself, then laughed even harder because I knew I was delirious. That joke wasn't even funny.

Bath time, then bed. Crap. Did I give the guys the code to get into the building? I'd better wait for them.

I took off my shoes and tossed them in the garbage can. They were absolutely ruined.

Both showers were being occupied at the same time.

Looks like I won't be taking that bath for a while.

Next time I moved, it would be wise to get a place with three showers and four bedrooms. A place like that would cost an arm and a leg in Seattle.

Too bad we all couldn't just move the Witch's House here. That place had rooms and showers coming out the wazoo, and I wouldn't mind seeing Mrs. Spigot's face after a night like last night.

Carter

Jareth rang the buzzer to Amira's condo, but no one answered. I panicked until I heard her sleepy voice come over the speaker. "Come on in, boys."

Buzz.

Up we went. Just in time. A woman going into her condo closed the door right as we passed. If she'd seen the state of us as we walked through the security doors, she'd have called the police.

We were beat up, bloody, and looked like we needed medical intervention.

Well, not me, of course. I looked the best out of all of us. I glanced at the other two guys and counted my blessings.

Somehow, I'd come out of the whole situation completely unscathed.

Jareth's neck had turned a bluish-green as it bruised over. The impressions from each digit of the witch's fingers stood out in stark relief—clearly visible for all to see.

Max was absolutely covered in dried blood from his nostrils to his lower chest.

Yeah, we needed to get inside Amira's place. Stat.

Otherwise, someone was going to call the cops, and we'd have absolutely no excuse.

Why did the driver even let us into his car?

That question was dispelled when I remembered the way his car had smelled. It was several years' worth of thick, pungent layers of skunkweed.

We stood in front of Amira's door. Jareth's hand was raised to knock as it swung open. I knew Amira was absolutely exhausted as soon as I saw her face.

"Welcome back, boys." She eyed us up and down, one by one. "You look like hell. Get in before anyone sees you. Goddess knows I can't handle any more crazy today."

She stood aside to let us in. Jareth grunted and trudged into the room. Max headed in and disappeared around a corner.

"You didn't happen to bring my laptop, did you?" I could tell from the tone of her voice she was only half joking. That tickled me no end. Only Amira could wonder about work property when she was in the aftermath of an impossible situation that bent the rules of reality to damn near breaking.

"Well, as a matter of fact, that's how I happened upon your friends."

Her face fell.

It took a second to register she most likely interpreted that as me having brought the laptop and lost it along the way. She wasn't jaded enough at her job to come to the natural conclusion I'd followed her home.

This might get awkward.

"Damn. No idea how I'm going to make partner after losing my laptop. The bag it was in had client files in it and everything." Her head snapped back and her eyes widened with guilt. "Not that I'm ungrateful for what you did, Carter. You saved our lives. Obviously, one laptop isn't worth the lives of my friends."

"And you," I said gently.

She smiled. "Glass of water?" She looked off toward a cabinet on the other side of the room. "Or maybe something a little stronger? I don't think anyone would judge us for a drink or six after what we've just been through."

We laughed.

The joke wasn't as funny as we made it out to be, but we were happy to be in a situation where we could laugh at all. "Water's fine."

She puttered off to the kitchen. I took the opportunity to snoop around and get acquainted, curious because I'd never been inside her place for this long.

I got a little antsy about what I should do after I finished the glass of water. Maybe I wasn't quite welcome here. With her and her friends safe at home, I was an interloper, a sixth wheel, but I didn't want to go back to my place and be alone. Not after what happened.

No. It wasn't that.

I wanted to be here for Amira on the off chance she

needed me. The strong Black woman trope that often existed as a need-based stereotype in an unfair world didn't mean she wasn't strong.

It just meant she'd been built tough in order to survive and achieve the level of success she'd garnered in such a short time. Deep in my heart, I'd always been there for her in ways she would never even know.

But I had to admit, it was so much nicer being there for her when she could actually appreciate it. Suddenly, I was saddened by the thought I'd eventually have to leave, regardless of the situation.

I didn't live here. This wasn't my home.

Amira walked in with a glass of water in one hand and a bottle of over-the-counter pain meds in the other.

"You don't look as ungodly beatdown as everyone else, but I brought these just in case." She poured two pills into my outstretched hand before sitting on the sofa and patting the cushion beside her.

I sat down obediently after taking the pills, sipping my water, unsure of what to say or do.

We sat quietly for quite some time. The only sound— snores and the hypnotic pitter patter of water from the showers in the background.

Jareth and Max were washing away the physical reminders of our previous encounter while Amira and I sat beside each other in comfortable silence. She lay her head on my shoulder and fell asleep. Her gentle breathing lulled me into a deeper sense of relaxation.

I joined her, hoping my snoring wouldn't rouse her from her slumber.

Amira

"I guess it's official," I heard Star say. Her voice woke me up out of a dead sleep. An uncomfortable dead sleep where I'd been left pitched forward in an awkward position damned near falling off the couch.

"What time is it?" I asked.

"A little after ten. Max went to get bagels. Flora and Jareth are still asleep. At least I think they're sleeping." She waggled her eyebrows naughtily.

I caught myself sighing in relief. The old Star was back. I was too tired to put much thought into why she was staring out the car window with that despondent and distant expression. But the brand-new day seemed to have reset her. She was back to normal now and in rare form.

Thank the Goddess.

I said a quick prayer in my head when she raised both hands to show me what I could only assume was a freshly brewed cup of coffee.

"Did you make that?" I wasn't able to mask the suspicion in my voice.

She shrugged. "Enough about my coffee. I can't give you food poisoning with black coffee."

"Black? You know I'm a cream-and-sugar kinda gal."

"Well, you're out of both. All you have in this house is liquor and brie. What was I supposed to do?"

"Um, wander downstairs and buy something from one of the five million coffee shops? This is Seattle, Star." Her reaction to my mock exasperation was an eye roll.

"It's winter." She plopped down in the chair across from me as I took a sip and curled my lip. She'd put something weird in it. "Whatever. Drink it or don't. I don't care. Tell me about this." She pointed a finger at Carter, who was passed out on the other side of the couch. Her pointed finger then moved to me and returned to Carter, going back and forth a few times.

"We're just friends."

"Very *special* friends. The knocking-boots kind. Girl, he saved us. I don't even want to know how or why he showed up there, but we would have been desiccated husks abandoned on a filthy warehouse floor if he hadn't shown up."

Carter smiled. Since he was obviously awake now, I dared to nudge him. "Star made coffee."

She flashed me a look I promptly put off by shrugging innocently.

Carter opened one eye and sat up. He grabbed the coffee with one hand, then put his other arm around me. "Maybe we should make it official?"

My face got hot.

"How about we table that discussion and continue after I get my laptop back?"

He chuckled, raising the mug to his lips. Winking at me over the brim, he took a sip and almost immediately grimaced.

"Okay, I'm not making either of you a coffee ever again." Star pretended to be mad for about three seconds before we all burst into laughter.

"Cooking isn't exactly one of Star's strong points. She does make a mean healing potion, but don't trust her around anything you intend to consume and derive enjoyment from." I gave her a pointed look. "And then there's the food poisoning."

If her glare were any sharper, it would have cut me to the bone. Maybe I'd pushed her too far.

"Noted," Carter said as he put the coffee cup on a trivet.

"Okay, he's a keeper. Any man who uses a trivet without having to think too hard about it is definitely someone to keep around," Star quipped before jumping up heading toward the front door.

"What are you doing?" The words slipped out before I had time to process them. If I'd thought about it, I'd probably have kept my mouth shut.

"Max is back, and I'm starving!"

"How did she know that?" Carter whispered when her back was turned. I ignored him.

Better to leave that up to the imagination. If he were sticking around for any length of time, he'd better get used to her "knowings."

That was what we called her precognitive moments when we were growing up.

Florebelle and Jareth joined us in the living room while Max was setting out the bagels on the coffee table. Star grabbed a handful of plates while I started a pot of proper Star-additive-free coffee.

The kind that didn't taste like watered-down battery acid and the bitter tears of our enemies.

As I brought over the mugs, I got a case of the warm fuzzies, seeing all my friends gathered around the coffee table.

Not only were we alive, we were also one big, happy family celebrating another glorious day together.

It couldn't get any better than this.

Chapter Twenty-Six

Amira

We took a couple days work off to recover and had a great weekend together. We wined, dined, and reminisced, but eventually, like all good things, it came to an end. Monday morning rolled around, and we reluctantly parted ways.

Carter left early in the morning, promising to bring my laptop to the office before any of the other employees got in and suspected anything.

That man was amazing.

I'd never been in a relationship where I felt so secure and happy. We were equals. He treated me well, seemed to dote on me, and best of all, these things extended to my friends. No, scratch that—he'd literally saved my friends' lives.

Talk about bonus points!

Not that a man had ever needed to go to those lengths before, but because he did, I could definitively state he'd more than earned his stripes.

Plus, as an added bonus, my besties absolutely adored him. He was affable and easygoing.

Easy to talk to and easy on the eyes.

Carter fit in well with the group. He even got along famously with Jareth and Max—whom I barely even knew. Over the short time they spent together, the three men became thick as thieves.

I strolled into the office at eight thirty, at least half an hour earlier than I'd intended, especially with not having a laptop to keep me occupied. Not having it was a mixed blessing, giving me time to work on a few tasks I'd been avoiding for far too long.

Five minutes into the spontaneous reorganization of my office, Carter popped in, laptop bag in hand. He surreptitiously peeked behind him to ensure there was no one in the hallway before giving me a quick peck on the lips.

We chatted casually while I docked my laptop and logged in. We idly prattled on about topics like the weather and our weekend plans. When my laptop connected to the Wi-Fi, I was quickly distracted by a slew of internal messages and emails popping up.

At first glance, more than half of the emails were from Susan. So, I did what I normally did when a client went completely bonkers with emails and opened the last one first.

Please stop by around 10:00 a.m. The executor will be here at 10:30.

"What the hell?" I hadn't meant to speak out loud. Carter came to stand beside me, face full of concern.

"Issue with a case? Should I head out, or can I help with something?"

He was too sweet. He'd always volunteered to shoulder the burden of my cases since the day I'd arrived. I didn't know why he was so generous.

Well, the reason for his kindness hadn't been apparent until now. My face must have lit up, because his concern turned to confusion.

"Oh, no. Well, yes. It's a case, but not necessarily a problem. The executor of the Price will is going to the house this morning."

"That's awfully fast, isn't it?"

"Yeah," I muttered as I read the email again, scrolling back up the thread to read the last few to glean more details. None of them had any information of any relevance.

Looked like I was heading to Denny-Blaine—the most expensive neighborhood in all the Seattle area.

"Wanna go snag a coffee before I head out to my client's place?"

"I don't know. We've been apart for what? Three, maybe four hours now? There's so much to catch up on. I might make you late." He winked at me as he turned away. "Let me grab my coat, and I'll meet you at the elevator."

My driver pulled up the Price mansion at exactly 10:22 a.m. I paid him and just stared, mouth agape, for another full five minutes.

The house was gorgeous. The lands were lush and green. I had dealt with several clients throughout the course of my time at the firm who lived here, but I'd never had reason to drive to the area.

A girl could get used to this.

I rang the bell, and a flustered woman in a classic, utilitarian, gray-and-white maid's outfit opened the door.

"Ms. Rapaport, here for Mrs. Price."

She waved me inside without so much as a greeting before

237

racing down a long corridor. I assumed I was supposed to follow and dashed after her so quickly, I wasn't even able to take in my surroundings. All I saw was wood and marble as we sped to our destination.

My heels made loud, rhythmic clicks on the marble floor as I jogged to catch up.

"Mrs. Price is right in here. Please ring the bell if you need anything."

I nodded, perplexed. She hadn't introduced me or anything, just left me beside a closed door.

Nothing to do but get this party started.

The meeting was pretty standard fare—completely uneventful. I didn't even understand why we'd needed to get together in such a rushed fashion. Surprisingly, no one was contesting the will and all the assets were in order. Mr. Halifax ran through the typical motions of an executor.

Susan just sat there nodding throughout the entire meeting, trying to keep her Cheshire cat grin at bay.

Long story short—she and her daughter got everything. Every penny. Every acre of land on every estate. Every speck of dust. All the i's were dotted and the t's were crossed.

Everything.

It was more than she'd ever dreamt of and was a complete one-eighty from two week ago. To be rid of the sadistic bastard and receive the whole shebang after thinking she'd lost her daughter and would become destitute?

No one could blame her for a shit-eating grin or two.

With the meeting concluded, hands shaken, documents signed, I deeply regretted the decision to drink the largest coffee in the world with Carter right before leaving for the Price mansion.

Once the bland, expressionless, gray-haired Mr. Halifax

shuffled off in his flashy suit and abundant jewelry, I felt like I could be myself.

"Susan, do you have a restroom?"

She was positively giddy when she replied. "A restroom? We have five in the main house last time I checked. And that doesn't even count the half baths, the pool house, or the sauna. Not even the cabana out back or the three bathrooms in the mother-in-law unit slash guesthouse."

She raised her arms above her head and twirled around happily while I crossed my legs and tried not to do the pee-pee dance in my client's mansion.

"Down the hall. First door on the left," she practically sang as she twirled.

Sweet relief!

As I sat on their imported Japanese smart toilet wondering if it was going to shoot water up my ass, I glanced down and saw a shining silver object at the base of the redwood cabinet. Once I'd washed and dried my hands, I bent to pick it up.

A cuff link with some kind of fish on it. No, it was a mermaid.

Why does it look familiar?

I brushed the nagging feeling off, figuring I'd give it to Susan on my way out. She could do with her ex-husband's belongings whatever she willed. I envisioned a raging bonfire near the tennis courts and chuckled to myself as I opened the door and made my way to bid farewell.

Those cuff links? I remember them now.

Stopping dead in my tracks, I felt like someone had punched me in the gut. The time I'd seen them, they weren't on Mr. Price.

No.

It was Carter.

I'd ribbed him mercilessly for wearing mermaid cuff links right before a deposition.

"Can't remember the last time I saw someone under eighty wear cuff links, but mermaids? You took it to a whole other level. Where did you even buy these?"

He became sheepish, not even responding, then left the room. His reaction made me feel bad. I thought maybe they'd been passed down by a dead relative and I'd been a righteous jerk.

Once I followed him out of the room, I went into work mode and promptly forgot about the whole situation.

I never saw or thought about those cuff links again until today.

It was possible Susan's ex-husband had the same pair. Better to hand them over and go about my business than to jump to conclusions.

"Thanks so much for stopping by on such short notice. Obviously, I can pay any extra necessary fees." Susan had stopped spinning like a whirling dervish and regained her composure.

"It was nice to visit this area. I've never been out here before. Your house is lovely." I held out my hand with the cuff link firmly gripped between my fingers and placed it on the edge of the tall mahogany display table she was standing beside. "Found this in the bathroom."

Susan picked it up and rolled it around in her hand. "Well, this isn't Sean's. He never wore cuff links. He was more into golf club chic." Susan chuckled wryly to herself. "I barely managed to get him to dress up for charity events. It was always a fight to get him to put on a button-up shirt." She sighed and absentmindedly handed the cuff link back to me.

My mind was racing so much, I didn't realize I was still

holding on to the small piece of jewelry until I was halfway back to the office.

I had two burning questions...

What business could Carter possibly have had with Sean Price? Why on earth would he drive all the way out there wearing cuff links, only to lose one in a bathroom?

My qualms about Sean's rather suspicious demise came back as if I were right there when we first learned the news of it.

Now, I was wondering about murder and questioning the only guy I'd let into my life in over a decade.

Why would Carter have been at the house? Sean was never our client. Were they friends? And how did he just happen to show up at the warehouse we were being held captive at, out of the blue? Was he a part of some crazy vampire conspiracy? Is there a conspiracy?

Maybe I was being completely paranoid, but I was going to have to talk to him about this.

And I wouldn't stop asking questions until I got answers.

———

As soon as I returned to the building and set foot in my office, Carter showed up. There was no point confronting him in the middle of the day. Instead, I opted to tell him I was super busy and waved him off. I sent him a quick email in the early afternoon asking if he wanted to get drinks after work. I'd learned long ago it was always a good idea to confront people in public places.

Internet rules apply: Don't know how someone's going to respond when you accuse them of murder? It's best to ensure you're around witnesses.

It's times like these I was extremely grateful I lived in a

secure building. I went through a mental inventory of my belongings and breathed a sigh of relief when I realized I hadn't actually left anything at his place. Since getting my laptop back this morning, I should be in the clear.

To be honest, I wasn't only relieved about not leaving my stuff at his place. Before our upcoming bleak discussion—which wouldn't end well no matter how this panned out—I'd hoped we might be something more.

Now, I could go back to the way things had always been. Yes, I might lose my work buddy, but at least there would be no maudlin sobbing into tubs of ice cream. No searching for answers in the bottom of my third bottle of merlot.

After he gave whatever excuses he could come up with, even if they were justifiable, he'd never look at me the same way again.

Despite the pit materializing in my stomach the moment I realized I'd never see those dark puppy-dog eyes full of adoration and what I now knew to be unrequited love, I couldn't let this drop.

I have to know, regardless of the outcome. Amira Rapaport is no shrinking violet.

Perhaps it wasn't as nefarious as murder. Maybe it was just him being in the wrong place at the wrong time?

If Carter was trying to poach clients or going behind the partners' backs—I was a horrible judge of character. A lack of ethics was something I couldn't abide.

There had to be not only an explanation, but also appropriate consequences. We believed in justice. At least I did. And betraying me and the firm? Let's just say that wasn't something I could sweep under the rug.

Especially with my impending partnership hanging in the balance.

Being made partner. Funny how Clements disappeared

when I was told I was being considered. His suddenly quitting seemed highly suspicious. Much more so now with Sean Price's sudden death on my mind.

I felt the hairs rise along my arms.

"Yeah, definitely gonna meet in public."

Carter

I almost glided into the bar, excited to spend another evening with Amira. It seemed like things had returned to their regular rhythm. Well, as regular as things might be, considering our budding relationship. I was almost giddy with anticipation. All the madness had been swept behind us.

Now we can create a better version of "normal."

Pushing my way through the cluster of people waiting to be seated, I scanned the bar for her face.

There she sat, glowing like a star on a pitch-black night. She was stunning, even after a long day at the office—well-fitting robin's-egg-blue suit, perfectly tailored to hug her body like a second skin.

I couldn't wait to peel off the layers of fabric, kissing her warm, smooth skin inch by inch.

She took a swallow from her glass before setting it down on the bar. It was obvious she hadn't seen me yet. I was a little disappointed she didn't look for me. It made me question if she was as eager to be in my presence as I was to be in hers. Those feelings didn't last long. Especially not when I slipped up behind her and pressed my body against hers.

"I see you started without me," I whispered into her ear. My voice sounded deeper and more gravelly than usual.

The feel of her body was difficult to ignore. I felt myself harden against her.

If we hadn't been in the middle of a crowded bar, I would have taken her then and there.

She turned slightly and pulled away from me. I didn't think much of it. In fact, I couldn't think much at all.

I took off my jacket, plopped myself onto the barstool beside her, and deftly draped the fabric onto my lap to hide my excitement.

With two fingers raised to the bartender, Louis, we made eye contact, and I dipped my head toward Amira.

Louis nodded and prepared our drinks.

"Now, where were we?" I asked as I pivoted on my stool to face her. When I saw Amira's face, I knew we wouldn't be heading back to my apartment any time soon. She looked like she was about to take on opposing counsel or grill a defendant on the stand.

She opened her hand, and I reached out to take it.

I glanced down and immediately stopped reaching toward her.

My stomach dropped.

"What were you doing at the Prices' mansion?"

My cuff link sparkled in the light reflecting off her empty glass.

I swallowed.

Hard.

Chapter Twenty-Seven

Amira

He sat, transfixed.

Carter couldn't take his eyes off the cuff link nestled on its bed of crumpled tissue that I held out in my defiant hand.

My hand didn't shake. I was proud of myself because I knew I exuded confidence in this moment. There wasn't the slightest tremor to show the rage and fear and whatever other indecipherable emotions lurked in the giant ball of growing nausea.

He just stared, unblinking.

Having deposed witnesses before, I could tell when someone was trying to think up a lie. The knot of emotions in my belly went from nausea to a burning flame. The desire to scream at him was building, but I took a deep breath instead.

This was nothing more than proof positive that my picker was broken.

After an eternity, Carter finally broke. "I was there."

My anger waned, and I was overwhelmed by waves of

regret. I sat unsure if I was disappointed more by the fact he told me the truth and I couldn't just immediately write him off as a liar or a murderer, or because by telling me the truth, I wondered if he always would be honest with me, no matter the consequences.

Few men would run through a gamut of emotions during a fight-or-flight moment and decide to acquiesce and just be honest.

"I don't know what to say to you," I admitted.

Guess who's the leaky sieve now?

"Look, Amira. I was there. But it's not what you think, I..." He wrenched his eyes away from the cuff link to look directly into mine. His eyes were lit with a fierce determination, shame, and a slight glimmer of hope.

Hope I won't turn him in or hope things aren't over between us? I might never know.

"You what?" I asked. My words dripped with the venom of disgust. My lip curled in a snarl as I closed my hand around the cuff link with force before letting my arm fall limply to my side.

"I need to tell you the *whole* story. You can turn me in to the authorities or whatever you want to do. Just give me a chance to tell you the truth. The whole truth. I need you to know what happened."

Carter lamely ended his sentence, and I was fine with that. I knew I should call the police and be done with it, but I was curious enough to hear him out. Besides, something deep inside told me he'd keep his word.

"Fine. Talk."

"Not here." Carter bowed his head like a beaten dog. The glimpse of him sitting there broken almost made me compassionate. Almost. He rubbed his temples and continued in hushed tones, barely audible over the hum of the bar's growing crowd. "Tomorrow. I'll tell you tomorrow."

"Tomorrow, then. And if you run..." The threat hung in the air, dense and ominous, but it didn't obscure anything—not his shame and certainly not my disgust.

"I would never run from you, Amira."

I couldn't take it anymore. It was too hard to look at him and think about all that had happened between us. Not just the amazing sex, but feelings of comfort and that I had so grossly misjudged him.

I'd been screwing a murderer. Entrusted him with my friends. Trusted him with my heart. This one was going to be hard to get over, but justice had to prevail.

The sting of tears made me jump up from my stool. Within moments, I was on the street. The tears didn't fall until I was halfway down the block and their flow was masked by a sudden burst of rain. A clap of thunder hid my sobs.

It was as if the very sky were crying with me.

Carter

How could I have been so stupid? Wearing those cuff links to the Prices' house and not noticing I'd lost one until it was much too late? So stupid!

Hell, I'd persuaded myself I must have left it somewhere else. That one mistake cost me everything. I didn't mind losing my freedom or material objects. The only thing I truly cared about losing was Amira.

Thankfully, my one saving grace was Amira agreeing to hold off on calling the police and listening to my side of things. As I sat alone at the bar, slamming the last of my fourth rum and coke, I couldn't believe she'd given me even that much of a reprieve.

Perhaps somewhere past the bitterness is the possibility of forgiveness?

It was more than I could hope for, but after hearing what I had to say, maybe, just maybe, she'd give me a chance.

She has to feel our bond. She just has to.

I held up two fingers. Louis nodded. It didn't take him long to set two more drinks in front of me.

Not having to drive home made getting shit-faced at a bar the best possible option. It could, after all, be one of the last times I got the chance to. Despite her feelings for me, Amira lived by the law. She saw justice as black and white. There was no way she was going to allow things to go back to normal after I confessed what had happened to her. I was damned lucky she agreed to hear me out at all.

A raven-haired woman slipped onto the stool, still warm from Amira. As the stranger swung herself around, her leg brushed against mine.

"Sorry about that."

I glanced at her. She wasn't sorry at all. She was flirting, and I wasn't interested. I shrugged and went back to my drink.

"You okay?"

"Yeah, I'm fine." Louis set my drinks in front of me, and I knocked them back as fast as I could before slamming the glasses down onto the bar.

"One sip'll do you," I said into the air, then I laughed drily. The woman held up a hand to tell the bartender to get me another of the same, but I shook my head. "Thanks, but no thanks."

She was taken aback. Her confident glint dimmed.

She was a stunner in a tight-fitting emerald-green dress

that set off her eyes and skin. This was a woman who wasn't used to rejection.

If it had been any other night, she would have pursued me further, but I got up and left the bar before she had the chance.

Amira

I collapsed on the couch, putting my dirty wet shoes on the coffee table. My black stilettos dripped Seattle street grime and Metro elevator piss onto my nice table, but I didn't give a shit.

My heart was broken.

Tears fell the entire walk home. I only took the Metro for a short stint, then ended up walking down the street I'd just been clubbed over the head and kidnapped from.

I was an enormous ball of the feels right now.

The powerlessness took my confidence down a peg or two. The strong Amira I'd built up over the years crumbled to dust.

Now, I was a little girl who knew she would never be loved. Even my parents gave me up without muss or fuss. Yes, my adoptive family of aunties loved me to pieces, but they had chosen me. Like picking a puppy out of a litter. They weren't made to love me.

They went kid shopping, and I just happened to fit the bill.

My biological parents hadn't even left so much as a note in a basket. Even Florebelle got a ring passed down to her from her mother. Something real and tangible to hold on to.

My phone rang, but I ignored it. Didn't even bother to

look to see who was calling. It was one of three people: Carter, who I refused to speak to on threat of death. Work, which I wasn't remotely able to face up to at the moment, being the emotional wreck I was. Or Star, with her psychic powers and impeccable timing.

The door buzzed. I ignored that too. Didn't even get up from the sofa to see who it was.

All the lights in my place were out, so there were no tell-tale signs from the street or hallway that I was home. Whoever was stopping by at this hour was likely up to no good.

Probably someone buzzing a bunch of condos, hoping someone would ring them up, thinking their food delivery had arrived.

They didn't stop.

Buzz. Buzz. BUUUUUUZZZ!

Anxiety high and getting epically annoyed, I stomped over to see who the hell was being this belligerent, only to see Star's face on the screen.

She was so wet, she looked like she was melting in the rain. Her braids were so soaked through, they were probably three times their normal mass. The thought of her wet hair being an extra pound or three made me laugh.

I didn't even say anything into the intercom when I pressed the button to let her in. She didn't speak when she set foot in the condo. All she did was wrap her arms around me in a giant, bone-crushing bear hug. She didn't let go, and I relaxed into her. All the bundled-up tension released.

Star was my rock.

As flighty as she might be on occasion, she always showed up at the exact right time and always did the exact right thing. There was no point in asking how she knew. Whether it was intuition or she read it in the cards, the one thing I knew was that Star was always there for me.

I sobbed while Star wrapped me in her arms. She was silent and stoic and full of love.

If her hair weighed more from being saturated by the rain, I wondered how much my tears added to her burden.

I woke up next to a sprawled-out Star, arms and legs spread wide, taking up more than her fair share of the bed, happily snoring away. She never woke up while I got ready and slipped out of the apartment.

When I was halfway to the garage, I thought to text her: *Will be back in a couple of hours. There's half a quiche in the fridge.*

It was a preventative measure to keep her from trying to cook anything while I was gone.

Discovery Park. One of the largest parks in Seattle.

Why I was going out into the boonies alone, to meet a man I know recently murdered someone, was beyond me.

Carter would never hurt me.

If there was anything in this world I was absolutely sure about, it was this one thing.

The knowledge wouldn't keep me from doing what was right. He had to pay for his crimes.

The driver let me off in the near-empty parking lot. I didn't know what to do next. This place was enormous, and Carter hadn't exactly given me directions. My phone pinged. He'd texted me the coordinates.

"What the hell?"

A woman gave me a dirty look as she slammed her car door closed and dragged her young child away. My early morning cursing must have pissed her off. I felt bad and gave her an apologetic look before saying, "I'm sorry.".

She turned to give one more pointed glare, pursed her lips, and continued on.

Apology not accepted.

I realized I'd need to open Google Maps and hope it could give me directions based on longitude and latitude.

Like this was some kind of goddamned treasure hunt. The prize coming when the police arrived and hauled my lover off to jail.

It worked.

Copying and pasting the coordinates produced the desired results. I was half hoping it wouldn't, but I had no excuses left.

I reluctantly made my way to him.

"Why are we meeting on a cliff? Should I be worried?"

Carter faced the water, looking far past the distant waves. With his back to me, I wondered if my voice was carried away on the wind, because he didn't turn around to acknowledge me. Or maybe he was trying to think of what to say.

My gut churned when I realized when he did finally move to face me, we'd be at the point of no return.

How do we ever come back from this?

Despite telling myself it was over, I still held out hope he could somehow convince me of his innocence.

"This is my favorite place."

Not knowing what to say, I remained silent, but slowly made my way to him. I was drawn to him in this moment, yearning to reach out and put a reassuring hand on his shoulder.

I felt compelled to comfort him because he was only doing this for me, so I could have closure. Neither one of us really wanted it. Once the words were spoken, they could never be taken back. When you know the truth, you *have* to act on it.

Indecision is still a decision.

We stood shoulder to shoulder, gazing out at the water together.

"I didn't mean to kill him. Sometimes..." His Adam's apple bobbed up and down as he swallowed. I couldn't tell if he was nervous or trying to hold back tears. "Sometimes we just don't know our own strength."

Chapter Twenty-Eight

Carter

I could feel her presence beside me, but I couldn't bring myself to look at her. To face her.

It was time to tell her what had happened.

This would be the final straw that would break us. A point of no return that ended what I'd spent so many years dreaming about.

She could never love me after this.

"I went to the house to get him to confess to manipulating the system for sole custody of his daughter. He just wanted her to spite his ex-wife."

No, this isn't how I should start this. This is the cowardly way.

I turned to face her. To see her bathed in the sunlight of a new day so I could capture this one last mental picture of us together. Something I could cherish and cling to for the rest of my long life.

This will be how I remember my beautiful Amira.

"I've always loved you, you know? I heard you singing in

255

the break room on your first day at the firm. That was the moment I decided to go to law school, because I wanted to be your equal. I wanted to protect you. I wanted to..." My voice caught in my throat. "You reminded me of home, and that made me think I might not be so alone in this world."

Fuck.

I was losing her.

Judging from the way she was looking at me, she thought I was some kind of stalker.

"None of that matters. It's time to set you free." The wind picked up and rustled the dying blades of grass around us. "I sang to him. To get him to change his ways."

Amira's face was a mask of confusion. *She still doesn't know.* "In the song, I told him he was a worthless monster who didn't deserve to live. After I left, he washed down a bunch of pills with liquor."

"What are you saying? Carter, how could you be responsible for a guy taking a bunch of pills by singing a song to him and leaving?"

She's acting like I'm crazy. How can she be in so much denial?

"Dammit, Amira. How can you be so blind?"

She cringed, stepping away from me. It was like I'd slapped her in the face.

How can she still have no idea? She's still blind to the things she's seen and done and refuses to accept the reality of the world around her. Or she's under a spell. Someone's trying to keep her safe. Hidden even from herself? That means she'll never be able to understand what I've done.

I wanted to reach out and hold her one last time. To pull her inside my head so she could experience all the memories and thoughts I'd ever had about her from the moment I saw her alone in that break room, singing a soothing lullaby to herself. A song I heard often as a child.

She meant more to me than life itself, but we were over now.

Amira thought I was crazy. She didn't know what I was talking about, despite all the signs. Despite an entire life with all the answers laid before her. She wasn't like me, but she was, all at the same time, and I loved her all the more for it.

The one thing I couldn't do was face the consequences of my actions without knowing she understood. Knowing she never would was a punishment worse than death.

"I can't do this." My heart felt like a lead weight in my chest.

Amira

"I can't do this."

Before I had time to respond, I knew he was about to do something stupid.

The world went into slow motion as Carter's legs bent. His thighs almost burst the seams of his too-tight pants. With a great upward thrust, he propelled himself over the edge of the cliff.

I couldn't gasp. I couldn't scream. All I could do was watch as he plummeted into the crashing waves below.

Scrambling to the edge, I felt more than heard a great grunting cry escape my throat.

Before I knew it, he was gone.

I tried to stand, but my foot slipped on the wet grass. The earth was no longer below my feet. The intensity of the sensation grew as my stomach dropped the way it does when you're plunging down, down, down on a roller coaster ride. My ears hurt from the whistling rush of wind.

All I could see before me was a lifetime of regrets.

Regret I'd never gotten therapy for being abandoned by my parents. Regret I'd never shown appreciation to my aunts for taking me in. Regret at the pain Star and Florebelle would feel when they found out what happened to me.

Is that deafening sound the wind... or my screams?

Please, Goddess, make this a merciful death.

There would be no mercy here.

The frigid ocean spray rose to greet me right before I felt the crushing blow of my body hitting the water. It felt like smashing into concrete.

I was dazed from the impact. Even if I weren't being buffeted by the unyielding waves, I couldn't have caught my breath.

Trapped in the very thing I feared most in the world, I was smothered by terror.

I struggled like never before. The anxiety and pain of the fall itself were nothing compared to the searing pain that quickly overwhelmed every fiber of my being.

This can't be what drowning is like. It's worse than I ever imagined.

It felt like all the bones in my body were being systematically shattered within microseconds of each other. Every muscle fiber shredded and ripped away, leaving my nerves bare to the sting of the salt water now filling my lungs.

My legs.

My legs were melting away from a fire, hot as lava, that burned through the shreds of flesh, muscle, and bone. The earth-shattering pain shot through the core of me with a vengeance that wouldn't be stopped.

The Goddess was not merciful on this day. It hurt so badly, I prayed for death.

Florebelle and Star. No!

My death would hasten their own because the three of us were bound by the L'i'al Dool. If one of us died, there would surely be consequences.

The sides of my ribs split open.

I heard as well as felt it—a wet, resealable bag being unzipped.

Ice cold water flowed into my body, causing the pain to reach whole new heights. A pressure slowly building up inside me over this entire horrific experience suddenly released.

My death was a comfort.

There was no more flailing. The pain receded and grew distant. A calmness overcame me.

Maybe Florebelle, Star, and Mrs. Spigot can find whatever help they need to remove the curse, or at the very least slow it down. Perhaps they can find some other witch to bear the burden and relieve my friends of their dire destiny.

It was time.

Pain gone, I was ushered to the other side by a song. A most beautiful song.

It was a song I'd heard when I was a child. It was much louder now that my thrashing about had stopped.

The song told me to let go.

Goodbye, Florebelle. Goodbye, Star. I loved you both the most. Sisters forever.

I let the remainder of tension flow from my limbs, released the mental anguish, guilt, and shame built up in my mind over the past forty years, and breathed.

Accepting my fate and whatever was waiting for me on the other side...

I let go.

The entire world as I knew it melted away. I was left in a state of bliss, and it was glorious! I felt reborn. Renewed, and at one with myself in a way I'd never felt before.

I ran my hands over my sides and felt the gashes. They were smooth and tender. Their slick newness felt uncomfortable, like the skin under a blister being exposed to the air too soon.

The webbing between my fingers made me damned near piss myself. My entire body shot backward with a thrust of my tail from the shock.

My tail? What the hell?

I swung my lower half forward and examined my fins. Iridescent scales of blue, silver, purple, and green reflected the morning light that shone through the now-calming ocean.

Something reflective caught my eye in the distance. Whatever it was wedged under a rock.

Maybe, just maybe?

I tentatively moved my tail in a syncopated rhythm—one I was used to from years of swim team drills when I had legs.

Finding myself in front of the reflective object in a flash, much sooner than I expected, I was taken aback.

"Holy shit," I mused as I marveled at how easy it had been to swim that distance. If I had to guesstimate—which would be difficult considering I wasn't used to navigating oceans with a tail—I'd gone at least a mile in a couple of minutes.

My personal best in my heyday had been eighteen minutes. Which was why we won so many meets. If it hadn't been for my desire to go to law school, I would have trained for the Olympics.

I gingerly swam closer to what I had spied off in the distance. Just now, I realized I'd seen something a mile away underwater about as clear as if I'd been reading a book on my couch.

It was the windshield of a car. I shuddered to think of how it had come to be at the base of a cliff.

Not daring to look down into the murky depths of the water in case I saw something I would regret later, I positioned myself to get a view of my entire body.

My shirt was still on, but my pants were nothing more than a waistband speckled with shreds of cloth that rhythmically fanned out in the water with each thrust of my tail. I was battling the currents without thinking about it in order to stand still.

So crazy I could get accustomed to this so quickly.

I twirled around in a circle, keeping the mass of my body in the center, head craning to get as much of a 360-degree view as I could.

Despite the mind-blowing facts that I had a tail and could breathe under water—that I was a frigging mermaid—I was breathtakingly beautiful.

My fins were transparent and swirled around in the water like hypnotizing ribbons. Bluish-pink pulses of colors through the iridescence of my scales turned from blue to purple. The silver faded into a rosy copper tint, and the purple flashed even darker still.

It was a stunning effect.

I lifted my shirt to get a look at the cuts in my side. They were gills, pink and freshly made. The cool water was a soothing balm.

I took a deep breath and saw fluttering bubbles form within the chambers of my new lungs.

My hazy reflection darkened as the sun dipped below a cloud.

Somehow, in the brief darkness, my eyes adjusted, and I could see even better than before.

This underwater world was like nothing I'd ever experienced.

Once the sun had hidden itself, I could see and hear objects around me as pressure waves.

I can see with my whole body.

Overwhelmed by the surrounding beauty in this brief slice of time—a new sensation that brought me overwhelming joy—I sang.

The music was slow and awkward at first, but as my confidence grew, my song flowed more freely and my voice grew louder and stronger.

A joyous moment, marred by pain as my brain went from joyous to filled with unanswerable questions.

Why had my parents abandoned me? Why did I have to find out who I was like this? Would I be able to change back? Would I ever see my friends again? What do I eat? How do I sleep? What would become of me now that I was this...creature? Would I be alone for the rest of my life?

I cursed my parents for leaving me in a world where I would never be truly accepted. No wonder I spent most of my life feeling like a fish out of water. It was because I literally *was* a fish out of water.

The anger, betrayal, and loss burned, boiled up, and shot through my raw throat like bile. This was a manifestation of all the negative emotions I'd kept buried deep inside me over the years, pouring out and made real.

The song flowed free in a burst of tiny bubbles. Each one popped to reveal a note.

Discordant, haunting.

The water darkened even more as the clouds grew more intense. The very sun trembled behind its fluffy cover to escape my pain and rage.

I heard the waves pick up speed and crash violently against the rocks. The reflective glass from the car windshield shattered as it was pulled free from the claws of nature. Flung at breakneck speed closer to the cliff, it flew out of the water and crashed against the rocky base. Even though I was beneath the water, I heard each piece of shattered glass sink back into the sea.

The waves crashed even more brutally, and yet I sang on, unfazed.

It was a song of lamentation.

Chapter Twenty-Nine

Carter

Something was wrong. Very, very wrong.

An eerie feeling of danger crept over me as I swam as far and as fast as I could away from Amira. I tensed up to prepare for a fight. It was natural when we transformed, almost everything was a threat initially. The sea wasn't gentle, and her inhabitants took advantage of any weakness.

It didn't use to be this way, but so close to shore, we weren't quite the apex predators we became after being in our true form for a day or two.

I came to a dead stop, then whipped my tail at a sharp angle to spin and change direction. Whatever was coming was behind me. When I did my 180-degree spin, there was nothing there.

My spear was nowhere nearby. I hadn't gotten far enough out to sea to retrieve it. If it was still even there. It had been many months since I'd last swum in the ocean.

I wasn't completely defenseless, though. I gnashed my teeth and swung an arm—powerful on land, but ten times more powerful when I was in my natural element.

The skies darkened, the waters roiled, the waves crashed, and the frothy sea was frenzied enough to reach natural disaster levels. The back of my neck tingled.

This isn't natural. This is Amira.

Her song bashed against my eardrums like hammers, unyielding and hard.

Amira's song was the most powerful one I'd ever been present to witness. Even as a child, I hadn't heard one from so far away when the queen was defending us from the Kraken.

Amira's powerful and pissed.

I was off, tail swiping through the water like a precision blade, pushing me farther and faster than I'd ever swum before. Her call beckoned me on, and I exerted myself more than I thought my heart could take.

Breathless and heart racing, I stopped as quickly as I could in the stormy seas.

Floating about twenty feet away from her, I was held rapt in disbelief.

She was stunning.

With two legs, she'd been beautiful, but now that she was in her true form, she was art brought to life. The royal markings of silver, blue, and purple were mesmerizing. With each beat of her heart, the color intensified, then faded away. Her hair flowed out behind her, whipping frantically in the violent water as she floated in her power.

She's a diamond shining in the darkness.

Amira's pain and power were beyond measure. If I didn't stop her, she'd destroy everything surrounding us for miles.

A Song of Lamentation was no trivial thing for a typical

siren, but for one with such power? One whose voice could command the waves, the wind, and make the sun itself hide behind the clouds like a frightened child?

Emergency sirens were blaring on land.

I have to help her. This has to end now.

I opened my mouth.

Before I could get out a single note, I saw a cold, soulless, sapphire-blue flash of hatred in Amira's eyes.

A sonic wave hit me so hard in the chest, I was hurled backward head over tail with the air knocked out of me.

It was impossible to breathe. No matter how hard I tried to inhale, my gills wouldn't fill. They were paralyzed. My chest felt like it had been crushed by a monumental weight.

I was dying.

At least I got to see her in her true form. I always wondered what she would look like.

I was fading fast, but not ready to die yet. There was one last thing I could do to survive, though my chances were slim.

With a last burst of energy, I set forth for the shore. If I could just make it to the beach in time, I might be able to transform and heal. It was a long shot, but if I was careful with my energy reserves, I might just make it.

Slow and steady progress got me close to the shore. So close, I could taste it. I soon realized my plan wouldn't work. The weakness was setting in. Even if I got to the sands, there was no way I'd survive the transformation.

Fuck!

Amira

It couldn't have been him. That was preposterous. Carter hadn't magickally appeared in front of me with a look of concern and wonder on his face.

When I thought I saw a flash of him in my mind's eye—an illusion hovering in the water before me—my rage shot out and went hurtling toward him in the form of an expletive I'd never uttered before.

It *had* to be a figment of my imagination, because he was gone in the blink of an eye after the swirl of dirty water, debris, and bubbles cleared to reveal a vast open swath of nothing.

Nothing except my memories.

"You reminded me of home. You made me think I might not be so alone in this world."

The image of his mermaid cuff links flashed in my mind.

"What are you saying? Carter, how would you be responsible for a guy taking a bunch of pills by singing a song to him and leaving?"

I knew now exactly how you could kill someone with a song.

Tim Gramer, the school bully, pushed Florebelle from behind. She went flying forward before face-planting in a puddle, her pretty new blue dress covered in mud. I looked back at him in anger and sang a stupid little song, "Go play in traffic, Little Timmy Gramer. Get hit by a car. Couldn't make you any lamer."

All the kids laughed. The three of us walked home in silence, with Florebelle in the middle.

Four months later, long after we'd forgotten about what happened, Timmy Gramer returned to school in a wheelchair. He pissed himself when he saw me standing behind him in the lunch line. He turned so sharply to get away, he nearly tipped over in his haste and recklessness.

We never saw him again. Supposedly, he transferred to a different school.

My voice faltered.

It was right after that my aunties told me not to sing.

It seemed strange at the time. All three aunts met me at the bus stop, asking if I'd sung to a little boy at school. I said I wasn't sure. Aunt Coral's eyes pierced through to my soul with a stare so intense, I could almost feel her tickling my brain.

She sighed and gave me the first of many speeches on the short walk home. I only remembered fragments:

"We don't sing out loud."

A hundred other memories, not quite having such disastrous results, popped into my mind of me singing or humming something and the thing I most desired happening almost immediately afterward.

"You can hum, but don't use words."

"Never, under any circumstance, should you sing in anger."

Carter!

In my frenzy, I'd done the unthinkable. Sung the unthinkable.

"Just shove off and die."

Words sung in anger had real consequences. Dire consequences.

I frantically swam in the direction I last saw Carter's vague figure. My tail cut through the water like a knife, allowing me to glide with an accuracy and speed I'd never possessed when I had two legs.

My eyes strained to see as far into the distance as was humanly possible. If I hadn't been so caught up in trying to find Carter, I would have laughed at "humanly possible."

I wasn't human.

Being new to this, I didn't know how to figure out where he could have gone. I assumed he'd been pushed straight back. Perhaps the current had pulled him a different way?

Maybe he swam off in a completely different direction.

Pain!

My entire body was awash with pain. A thousand tiny needles.

I was led in a particular direction by something dire. It was definitely related to Carter. The sensation of suffocation washed over me. I convulsed in fear, thrashing against the water in terror.

I have to find him. Now! But where do I go?

Another surge. This time, it was overwhelming fear, sadness, and anger. It was hard, but I relaxed my mind and concentrated.

Where are you, Carter? I'm so sorry. I didn't know. Let me help you!

There.

A thread of light spun out in front of me. It was untouched, unaffected by the ocean's natural movements. Without questioning it, I followed the cord as fast as I could.

If I thought I swam fast before, it was *nothing* compared to my adrenaline-fueled sprint to Carter.

My Carter.

Heart in my throat, I awkwardly pushed my body up onto the sand and landed with a wet, unceremonious thump beside Carter's motionless body.

"Carter?" I pleaded as I prodded him with a webbed finger.

He looked like he'd gone through a garbage disposal twice, then gotten spat back out again. He was half transformed. Toes peeked out from the tips of his tail—a blueish brown mashup of flesh and scales.

His gills were sealed shut, but his chest didn't rise or fall.

He simply lay there, flesh dry except for the spatter from the nearby waves that occasionally sprayed us both with salt water.

My body was heavy and foreign as I leaned over him, desperation fueled by torment at what I'd done.

I, too, was a murderer of sorts. Not knowing the power of my voice, I had sent him off to die.

"This is my fault. Carter, I—" My voice cracked. My head fell to his chest as tears poured from my eyes.

I sang like I'd never sung before.

The pain of my previous song was but a minor wave compared to the tsunami of emotion that poured from me in this moment.

Regret, and love, and pain.

The decisions I made in anger had consequences. Consequences I never could have fathomed.

I was a hypocrite. The worst kind imaginable.

All this, my transformation, my understanding of who I was, and murdering the man I loved.

If only I had been kept in my cozy web of lies and ignorance. Afraid of the ocean and not knowing what I was truly capable of.

I sang until my throat grew hoarse. Then I simply sang, unaware of the changes my body went through as my world condensed down to focus only on the man lying underneath me, covered in sand and the salty brine of my tears.

Tears flowed so heavily, they trickled down his face in thin rivulets that streamed into his mouth.

Carter

From the impenetrable darkness, I heard her call my name.

A sweet song that was just for me and me alone. Something I'd dreamt of since I first laid eyes on her, but never believed would be possible.

But here it was. Too late.

I had said my goodbyes.

Goodbye to a world I'd come to appreciate more than my brothers and sisters ever could. Walking on two legs among the humans had taught me many things. It was hard not to learn about the fragility of life when you lived among them for so long.

There were also the goodbyes I'd never given to the friends and family I left behind. Deep down, I'd always thought one day, I'd go back home to them despite the nature of my leaving.

And yes, I'd sometimes dreamt of returning with Amira swimming by my side.

She was there at my side now, singing a song for me, as I drifted farther away into the sweet current of the great below.

She called me back.

Something wrapped itself firmly around my waist, dragging me toward the faded, gauzy plane of the realm of the living. I was powerless to fight it, I was so enthralled by her song.

I can't leave her like this. So hopeless. So alone.

After passing through the barrier between worlds, there

was salt on the tip of my tongue. It tasted like the purest essence of the sea. I took a faltering breath and squeezed out a single note. It flowed in time with hers, entwining around it like a living thing drawing its other half close. Like a snaking vine that wove in, around, and through all the nooks and crannies to create unbreakable knots of such intricacy, it was impossible for the eye to follow.

With each note, I grew stronger. My voice grew stronger.

We created a powerful sound mightier than that of the blue whale. The song's power surged through me and helped my body complete its transformation.

My tail split.

The skin peeled back and sloughed away, leaving me a complete, unbroken man.

I reached up and cupped Amira's chin in my hand. I sang louder, beckoning her to sing with her full voice. As beautiful as this moment was, I knew she was holding back.

Our eyes locked. Amira's irises sparkled with the same silvery blue, pink, and purple colors of her tail. When she smiled at me, the full power of her magicks was unleashed. Time stopped, but we did not.

We sang of the past, the present, and the future.

We sang of togetherness and to never being alone.

We sang of forgiveness and understanding.

We sang of life, death, and every moment in between.

And then, when we were full to bursting, caught up in the glory of the moment, our very souls calling to each other, we touched our foreheads together and stopped on one, sweet, lingering note that hung in the air for several seconds before we synched back into the flow of time in the world surrounding us.

The storm passed. The sun no longer hid behind the clouds. Birds chirped cheerily. The world was once again bright, shiny, and new. And the sea? She was calm and smooth as glass, reflecting the sky above like a mirror.

I barely saw any of it. I only had eyes for Amira.

Her head dipped down to kiss me. It was salty and sweet, still tinged with the lingering residue of our mingled magicks.

Chapter Thirty

Amira

"Thank the Goddess you had these stashed out here. Do you do this often?"

"Often enough to realize having clothes hidden in prime locations is a smart move."

Carter wrapped the wet towel around his neck.

We looked ridiculous in our mismatched clothes. Mine were particularly bad because they were several sizes too large, but I was grateful because it was a lot better than ending up in jail on indecent exposure charges.

I giggled like a schoolgirl as I stood, hand firmly gripping the waistband of my bright yellow shorts lest I end up half-naked on the beach.

"Okay, let's head to your car. I need a hot shower and a hot minute to process all this."

He held both ends of the towel draped around his neck. "Amira?" His voice was soft.

Is he about to break some bad news to me?

It sounded like Carter was ramping up to tell me something I really, really didn't want to hear.

"Yeah?" *Please be something like he lost his keys in the ocean or something.* "Oh shit. My keys?"

"Don't worry about your keys right now. There's something I need to tell you."

The cold ocean breeze made his hair dance. It was the only thing moving as we stood staring awkwardly at each other.

I wasn't prepared for any more news. All I wanted was to go home, take a hot shower, and tell my friends about my crazy-assed day.

Will the drama never end? I'm pretty sure this is just the beginning of my drama.

"It's about the merfolk and sirens. I left because I was sick of the constant infighting between clans. I decided to live with the two-legs." He corrected himself. "Humans. Your particular tail coloring means you're probably from a pod near Atlantis. Royalty. They have a tendency to abandon children deemed inferior or weak, but that doesn't make sense. You're one of the strongest sirens I've ever seen."

I was in shock, unable to process what he just said. "That was something of an info dump, Carter. Not really sure how to respond to this." I turned to face the ocean. "Maybe we can hold off on all that for a bit. Let me come to terms with what I already know. It's plenty enough to deal with. I don't need to add more parental baggage to the equation."

"Yeah, I guess it would take time after finding out you're not quite who and what you thought you were. Just know that if you ever want to look into it or talk about it, I'm here for you."

He gently caressed my cheek, sliding his palm under my

chin. Taking a step forward, Carter kissed me so deeply, my knees buckled, and I nearly fell.

But he caught me.

"Let's go back to my place. We can take a shower and grab something to eat. I'm feeling like sushi. Do you want sushi?" I asked.

We chuckled as he slipped his large warm palm into my hand and drew me farther up the beach. Hip to hip, we walked back to the parking lot. I leaned into him as he bent over to kiss the top of my head every few steps.

The smell of his skin coupled with the sunlight and salty tang in the air was perfection. I felt as if I'd been made whole.

We did, in fact, stop for sushi on the way back to my place. My keys and cell phone had been lost to the sea, but Carter had a bundle with everything he needed stashed nearby.

He was my big, burly Boy Scout.

Star buzzed us in and dragged me inside as soon as I got to my condo door.

It might have been more pleasurable to have drowned in the ocean, because she almost smothered me to death with her ample bosom in one of her patented bone-crushing bear hugs. This one was particularly enthusiastic.

"Star. I...can't...breathe!" The words came out in a sharp staccato in between painful squeezing rounds.

"I'm just so happy!" She squealed in delight. "I felt you dying and your heart breaking, but I couldn't see the outcome."

"She can feel when things go wrong, but can't clearly see her own future or those of the people she's closest to. She just gets flashes that are hard to read," I whispered to Carter.

"Well, you're here, and Carter's here. Everything's going to be great." She turned somber. "Maybe not great, but things are good for now. And that's the best we can hope for."

"You got that right, sis," I said with a wry laugh as I made my way to the bathroom. I paused before passing through the doorway leading into the hall. "Are you coming?" I seductively waggled my eyebrows at Carter.

He made his way toward me with a hungry look in his eye.

As we rounded the corner and made our way to the bathroom, I heard Star laughing to herself. "Go have fun, you crazy kids. I'll see myself out."

***

The water was skin-scorchingly hot. Steam filled the entire bathroom within minutes. We stripped down, and I slid under the delicious cascade of heated water.

"I hate to ask this, but how do merfolk have sex? I didn't really have much time to check out the anatomical differences between us." I asked innocently, Carter's smile faltered and turned sheepish. "Well, maybe we can save that lesson for later."

"Looks like I'll have to show you a lot, but you made it through law school, so you're undoubtedly a very fast learner."

"Perhaps. But, right now, I need you to reeducate me on the finer points of making out."

I grabbed his hand and drew him under the spray of water blasting from above and the two sides of the shower enclosure.

"Damn, this is nice."

"Oh, if you think this is nice... Alexa, Ocean Relaxation mode."

The lights turned blue and pulsed rhythmically. Sounds of the sea rose like the sweetest music around us. Recordings of whistling whales and dolphin clicks would forever sound fake and shallow to me now.

"So..." I said as I gazed up into his soft eyes.

"So..." he replied as he picked me up, swung me around, and pressed my back against the cool tiles before planting another deep, luscious kiss on my lips.

It wasn't long before our ecstatic moans made music as beautiful as any siren song.

About the Author

About Stephanie:

When USA Today Bestselling Author Stephanie Berchiolly's not writing novels and screenplays, she's spoiling her bird, Peppers, rotten, providing endless jump scares for her partner, Rick, or baking wackadoo things like cakes with pies inside.

But Wait, There's more!

To learn more about Stephanie and what she's getting up to please visit: **stephanieberchiolly.com/learnmore**

To hear all the latest news about Stephanie's new releases in the *Scenic Magical Midlife Tour* series and be notified of sales, make sure to subscribe to her newsletter: **Sign up for Stephanie's Newsletter**

To join **Stephanie Berchiolly's Facebook Reader Group**

Review This Book:

Please let others know how much you loved this book by leaving an honest review with the vendor you purchased it from. Reviews are the lifeblood of authors because they help spread the word and increase sales which, in turn, allow them to write more books for you to enjoy.

This is the circle of life for authors and readers, and increases the chances of us writing more books for you to love! *Thank you!*

- amazon.com/Stephanie-Berchiolly/e/B07JGJMC3F
- bookbub.com/profile/stephanie-berchiolly
- goodreads.com/stephanieberchiolly
- facebook.com/SBerchiolly
- tiktok.com/@stephaniebauthor
- instagram.com/stephanie.berchiolly

Made in the USA
Monee, IL
30 August 2023